WITW*ORTHD*OO*M*

BABY

A PAST AND FUTURE ACCOUNT OF THE END OF
THE HIGH WITCH WAR AND FALL OF HUMANITY
AS RECORDED BY THE IMMORTAL COURT

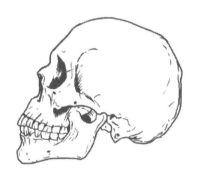

Stefanie Simpson

Published by Stefanie Simpson
© 2020 Stefanie Simpson

Cover design © 2020 Stefanie Simpson. Image from Unsplash.com

CONTENTS

This is a book of death and the love bound in it. It is not a tale of mortal love or a short blinking existence; it is of eternal spirits moving beyond mortal woes. Everything ends in this book. There is no rescue for humanity.

Reader, you will not be saved.

△ △ △

CONTENT WARNING: This book contains parental death, estrangement and grief. Pandemic loss of life. Bloody violence and gore. Sexual content and strong language. Coercive and manipulative organisations. Fire and Arson. References to unwanted pregnancy. Supernatural horror.

For the outsiders and those who never fit in anywhere.

INTRODUCTION
by Micah Chaim Thomas

Goths. A subculture spun off from Punk, surviving within waxing and waning enclaves across the globe, characterized by gloom and dark intensities in fashion, music, art, and lifestyle.

Gothic Literature. A genre predating society Goths, characterized by tragic romance, secrets, lush textures of a fallen grace, an aftermath of hubris, survivors and ghosts, and ethereal otherworldliness.

Witworth Doom Baby is both Goth and Gothic Literature. In the spirit of Poppy Z Brite, Anne Rice, China Miéville, and the White Wolf Publishing, *Vampire: The Masquerade*, Simpson completes the last leg of the journey through the underworld and returns us to the 1990s before catapulting the genre into new ground.

Genre writing is something Simpson knows well having authored many well-received Romance novels and stories. The rule set for writing in genre is predicated on creative use and subversion of established tropes and mechanisms to simultaneously provide a genre reader with familiar dramatic irony and setting, while also delivering surprise and delight in the fresh construction. This is challenging work. Too much familiar, and readers sense the formula and cry, "It's too predictable!" Too little, and readers, looking for the fulfilment of genre promises, grow alienated. This is baking. This is chemistry. One can easily overwork the dough or have a character growth fail to rise in the oven. Simpson, however, is an alchemist of narratives, combining base materials in such precision as to transmute the common into the sublime.

How though? How does Simpson combine Goth subculture and Gothic Literature into a fresh, yet familiar, story? For this reader, it started with a well-grounded universe delivered through controlled touch world building. Doom Baby didn't data dump me into Witworth Manor. I entered, running my fingertips over old wood, smelling ages of smoke embedded in heavy curtains, and feeling my back up against the wall with Adaline when confronting ageless frenemies. I *knew* who the main character was, even though I didn't know what she was. I *knew* where I was and I was afraid of that place! Personal dread, ghosts, antagonists, and an ineffable horror lurked within!

In terms of Gothic horror literature, in its deep roots, Edgar Allen Poe provided fertile and bloody ground for our seeds to grow. In this ground, Simpson evokes the time-honoured pressures of rising dread, ancestral taint, corruption, and the ruination of an ancient charge. Yet, many authors in genre fail to eclipse the limitations of one who once said, "The death of a beautiful woman is, unquestionably, the most poetical topic in the world." Here, Simpson turns the wheel forward. We are not fretting about over a CIS romance, nor is our dread a father proxy for a cruel and negligent God. No. This is a female story. Mother is the name of our ghost and that relationship is haunted with the bonds of love and fear as real as any abusive family chain. We are not following a man pining over the death of a woman, but a woman taking agency, fallible agency, over her body against the internal and external forces seeking to police or manipulate her. Does that sound like social critique? Because that's how I read it. But still, true to Gothic form, the heavy weight of legacy exerts gravity as much as the name Usher and the fall of that house. Remember this point later.

So, we Goth on, heavy coat, taking refuge in its depths, pockets like a Bag-of-Holding, producing lollies and smokes. The attraction of death, Eros and Thanatos, hangs in the air. In lesser hands, the dynamic between "I mustn't join the dark side," and "Oh, but isn't it nice," can fall into Bathos, a la Louis in the Vampire Chronicles. Here, we find no such lapse into unintentional comedy because Simpson grounds the tension in real human conflict. Not an abstract good vs evil. No, we find duty to self vs legacy vs the seductive influence of letting go of worry and allowing the monster within to completely possess you. The id is so strong. The power and fire calls to the Goth heart as when Lili danced with Darkness in the film Legend and wee Goth kiddos shouted, "Do it! Join him! Look at that dress you get to wear!"

There is more, though, than Goth and Gothic thread in Doom Baby's tapestry. Beyond the black rainbow of genre and subculture, Simpson takes off her gloves and feeds us psychedelic words with the care of an administering shaman. Simpson writes a compelling trip into altered states of consciousness. I *saw* a detachment from the flow of data — scene/relatable/tangible. I *experienced* a psychological/emotional/spiritual exploration as only could have been done by a master artist. This leap into the unknown comes through literary magic but makes its home within the diegesis.

Sublime. Difficult. Challenging. Transgressive. The choices Simpson presents should make you think. While a pleasure read, there are questions and hypos in both narrative structure and in the story which you should think about. You should close this tome while wearing all black, perhaps a Clove cigarette burning itself out in the ashtray, turn up the volume of the Cure or Rasputina, and let the darkness permeate in your skin.

A PRÉFACE TO THE DOOM

Foweller's texts tells us much of our lore and history, and I could recount it all here, but they're very dry and kinda dull. Besides, when I think back on those times, it is with grief, and what matters are the small stories of each of us who played a part and make up the whole of what took place.

The Court Library is a vast record of our history where older, loftier minds have pieced together the days of The Great Death. It was quick and brutal. It took all and spared few. These are the words enshrined in our records. But that isn't the story I'll give you, and I could give you mine, yet this, for reasons you will learn later, means a great deal to me. Other, lesser tales are here because they belong nowhere else. This is the book of unwanted and outside tales. Here, in the great atrium, at a desk, while birds sing and it is both spring and autumn in continual harmony, I can forget the sacrifice of others. And here, compiling a history of death to come, I am reminded of all that was lost. I see her eyes at night. Her voice is a dream I long to keep close and forget. A bittersweet depth of hard angles and soft kindness.

And I'm the record keeper of her truth. I transcribe and write. Sometimes I weep.

This is not a mortal tale; humanity fell. Death came. There was no salvation for you. Love? Yes, perhaps, the one person above such traits loved when it mattered. What is that love? A child in a parent's arms? Sex? An act of kindness for your enemy?

I do not answer these questions; I do not know the answers, I am more than fifty now, and have no idea beyond thoughts I can't articulate.

I could tell you the meanings of what's to follow in a small way but won't, I'll give it to you as it was told to me.

Truth or not, it's honest to her.

DON' T MOURN ME, I SAID, FOR THE DEAD DON' T DIE

Mother was dead. I stood on the back porch watching a bird peck at brown grass, letting that remarkable fact sink in. The house was exactly the same as it'd always been with decay and death hovering. It saturated the walls.

Memories bit and reeked, and I remembered how mother paced the deck at the back of our little house. She stamped up and down, making the wood creak and groan as she passed in front of the window. When her face appeared, my heart would skip a little, and then I'd breathe again, my small body flooded with fear.

Pace. Pace. Pace.

That was long past, and nothing remained of that time other than my memory, and even that was unclear.

Autumn always brought bitter wind, and it whistled through the house as I turned from the garden and faced the building. Some of the decking had rotted away over time, and I huddled in on myself, nudging the broken wood with my foot.

The past tumbled in with all the things I'd stored away in a box with a lock on it. In the wake of her death, it opened. I ran my fingers through my hair and the impulse to keep walking itched. Out to the wood, golden and red, the browning fields, and fallow ground. It struck me how dead the garden was. Everything around the house was winterised. Not the earthy joy of autumn, but the dead January of winter. Blackened decay.

My teeth chattered.

My mother's name hovered on my lips. My tongue itched to say it, but I didn't and went inside.

She lived like a monk. The same furniture dotted about, and same plain dull walls. A childhood nightmare realised.

Here I was right back where I started.

In the middle of the room, on the same dirty rug where I used to sit and watch her pace, I looked down, swallowing bile. A beetle, shiny and dark, trundled along, going about its business.

It deserved better.

I squatted and scooped the little thing up. It curled over my palm, and I turned my hand. Walking out the back door, I went into the air, breathing deep, and set it down on a dead leaf.

"Adaline Greyling?"

"Yes." I turned to the figure that appeared in the doorway, brushing my hands on my coat. He was tall, with neat blond hair and darker stubble. Not obviously handsome, but he was appealing with a remarkably square jaw. I sniffed the air, and he smelt like human, but almost too clean and pure.

"I was left instruction to meet you here."

"And you are?" I waited at the bottom of the steps.

He smiled, shaking his head. "How rude of me. I'm Edward Church."

"Mr Church." I put my hands in my pockets, wondering what he was.

"Were you not expecting me?"

"No. I just came to see the house, though I'm not sure why I did." I screwed my face up against the wind.

The pensive man came down a few steps. He was debating what to say to me, and I was pondering how hard it would be to break his neck.

"I was asked by your mother's solicitor to come and see you when you said you were coming up." Mr Church looked heavenward as the first spots of rain fell. "Shall we?"

"I don't mind the rain."

In the silence, he waited for questions, for my grief, for the things a man who didn't know me would expect me to say.

I didn't even blink.

"There are questions." He waited. The rain pattered. "About what happened. About you."

"Are you police?" He felt like a trap.

"No. Not strictly. I'm an investigator."

I wondered what sort. Perhaps the kind that killed my kind. Hunters. Servants of what I stood against, not that it was that simple. "What a tedious occupation that must be for you."

He seemed surprised. The rain came heavier, and he popped his collar up. "Can we get out of the weather?"

I looked at the door, and he went up. Back wool coat, black suit. Grey tie. The only interesting thing were his good shoes.

"Are they handmade?" I stared at his feet.

"Yes. It's hard to get good shoes in my size."

"Expensive. Is that why you skim everywhere else?" I let my eyes wander down his perfectly nice form.

He laughed, looking down with a blush. My skin goosed.

I glanced back to the woods, still irritated by the impulse to walk out to it. "Mr Church, what is it you think I can do for you?"

"Your mother's estate is yours. There was a sizable insurance policy on her life. But upon her death, there are some strange caveats."

That didn't ring true. "She was a strange woman."

"The caveats are about you."

"Of course." The rain stopped, leaving damp air. I scrutinized him and wondered what he knew and how much I would have to give him to make him go away. "Do you know what she used to call me? The Doomer." I watched for his reaction, any hint I'd have to fight, and where he stood in the war.

"Excuse me?" He looked baffled by the term, but that didn't mean he was harmless. I took a deep breath, taking in his scent. No, he was very human. Merely a pawn by the look of him. Just my type too. Shame. I hadn't had a good fuck in months. All the delightful things I could do with him flashed through my thoughts, but I shook them off.

"She was outright convinced I was here to herald the end of all things. She'd weep and wail. She locked me in this prison. She nearly ended my life. My aunt, her sister, came for a surprise visit since she disappeared off the face of the earth, and found me. Silent, pale, numb. I was eleven. She took me away. I don't remember any of the details, the how or why. None of it. I remember I was playing in the garden, and then I left."

Mr Church looked aghast. No, he wasn't one of them, but he wasn't innocuous; human pawns were as dangerous as any supernatural creature.

"You can check my history. I didn't exist until I went to school. It was a bad fit. I haven't seen or talked to my mother for twenty years. I get a random phone call telling me she's dead and it's all mine. Suddenly, I'm supposed to care. I don't, Mr Church. At all. I'm done. Burn it to the ground for all I care." I shrugged and went inside, and that damp decay made my sinuses itch.

"It's not that simple."

"I imagine it isn't. Check up on me and, if you can, find me."

The back bedroom was completely bare other than for a cupboard against a wall, yellowing wallpaper peeling from the damp, and mould crawling across the ceiling. My fingers twitched, and I opened the plain door. An old-style doctors' case was shoved at the back. I huffed at the bitter remembrance. Grabbing it, I marched out.

"Was your mother mentally ill?"

I dug my nails into my palm, swinging around. "No. She wasn't. That's an easy get out for people to rationalise the evil of others. It makes it easier for you to process. But mentally ill people are more likely to be abused than be the abusers. She was fucked up and a sadist. Not unwell."

I dropped the keys to the house on the front step and got in my car.

I shook, rigid.

He tapped the car window. "Apologies. I wasn't justifying her actions. Sometimes people do bad things without knowing what they're doing. Doesn't make them terrible people. I'm trying to understand."

I started the car and opened the window. "She knew what she was doing. She justified that by believing I was evil, but in reality, she used that excuse to rationalise resenting a child that ruined her life."

Tears burnt my eyes, and Mr Church nodded sharply and backed away.

What a gullible man.

STARK BL*é*SSI*N*GS A*N*D RU*N*G B*é*LLS

As I drove into the nearby town, something bothered me. I couldn't place the unease. I felt hasty and dangerous. Almost smiling, I glanced at the bag where she kept all kinds of secrets and magic. The memory of her rooting through it for something and glancing at me with fear flashed through my mind, but I shut it out. I zoomed along the roads, surrounded by farms and cattle, but pulled into a layby. Gripping the wheel, I took a few deep breaths. When I closed my eyes, I saw the woods beyond her cottage. I focused on the road and carried on.

What I needed to do next stole my impulsive nature. She'd not want me to do this, yet I was going to.

The old Victorian industrial town was virtually untouched by the modern world and felt decayed and forgotten. It was like a rotting tooth. The old brick hospital didn't look fit for purpose as I pulled into the barely paved car park.

Something about being at a hospital made me want to smoke again. I bought a pack from a newsagent's over the road and next to the funeral directors. How apt. On the cluttered counter were stacks of local newspapers.

Two local hikers were missing along with several sheep.

I blinked at their smiling faces, and that weird feeling that something was very wrong with all this got hotter. Tempering the impulse to burn everything, I paid the man at the counter and pocketed the cigarettes. He watched me with a dead stare.

Turning the packet in my pocket as I went into the hospital, I followed the signs for the chapel of rest. One of my gifts was seeing the dead, and they crowded the corridors in lingering echoes, not clear or with purpose, but impressions of existence. They hovered without consciousness and made my skin crawl. I hated hospitals. I arrived early, but the police officer, hat under his arm, was already waiting.

"Thank you for coming."

I nodded. "Is this also the morgue?"

"Yes. Small town. The police station next door is more of a booth." His smile was polite yet measured. A professional through and through. I took a deep breath. He was human. Not quite as pleasant as Mr Church — he was a breath of fresh air.

He gestured for me to go in, and we passed the small red curtained chapel of rest. Beyond it was a clinical room.

"You can stay behind the glass and view her from a distance."

"No, I need to see her up close. What were the circumstances of her death?" We went into the room. Sickly decay masked by chemicals and harsh light faded as I looked at the trolley. I expected her to sit up.

"She was found by some hikers in a field. Collapsed and already gone. Heart attack, the pathologist thinks. Did she have a history of heart problems?"

"I have no idea." She was over a hundred, but her exact age, I couldn't guess.

He took notes and was all authority and human uniform of guardianship. He had no idea how arbitrary it was, and what her death might mean, or who it was he led me to.

A bitter woman, abandoned by the world, shut in, and the kind of person who children whisper about. Harmless in human eyes, she was one of the most dangerous creatures on earth.

Someone in scrubs pulled down the pale green sheet, and I saw my mother's face for the first time since I was eleven.

I wasn't ready.

I clutched the things in my pockets and held everything in, but exhaled slowly, and the room's frigid buzzing warmed with my will.

She looked young. Small. Nothing like I remembered, but peaceful. I remembered her long wild hair and accidentally burning it when I reached out to touch it once. I could still hear her scream. I'd have been no more than five. As I closed my eyes, she paced the deck, sobbing and angry. The fear I felt wasn't always of her but of hurting her. Of being without her. The harsh light buzzed louder.

I wondered if her ghost remained and if she'd haunt the hills now. Wandering like other witches, left in a mortal realm and severed from our kind.

As long as she didn't haunt me.

The officer cleared his throat and wiped the sweat from his brow. I sought control, and the room cooled.

After I'd signed the paperwork, with promises to arrange a funeral and a dirge of human formality, I resisted the impulse to burn her body and left.

The drive to Witworth Manor gave me time to think. I hadn't been back in more than five years. It wasn't my home, and I knew if I went back, I'd be given up to the evil within it, exactly as mother was.

But I worked for Witworth Council, and they liked to keep me at a distance. The jobs they gave me weren't for the faint of heart, and for ten years I'd served them well, but the nature of the place was all levels of conspiracy and deception, so someone like me, with my reputation, couldn't be seen there.

I was the dangerous witch, the failure, so damaged by her mother that I couldn't serve Court or good society.

That used to make me smile, but not now. This was all wrong. I felt in my bones, my marrow liquid, blood stinging in my arteries, screaming danger.

Not because of what they'd ask, but the consequences. I had a vague notion of rippling damnation that would change everything. Though, I was often a little dramatic. I guess.

I didn't remember the drive but realised it was night, and my arse was numb. The giant oaks that rose at the end of the drive marking the entrance to the manor loomed in my headlights. I slowed, the engine ticking over. My skin goosed.

Time is funny for us. I was still so young to the older ones. They moved slowly, reacting with reflection to what happens. This, what was coming now, had been long planned. Slow moving cogs finally ticking into place.

I'd played along to survive, and I was one of those cogs, a small, fast moving one. Their plan became clear. I understood it, and my mother's unwilling role.

I remembered her face as I was snatched away from her.

"Every word is a lie. Undo it."

I said those words aloud. Undo it. She'd told me who I was, and the endgame. Few knew the truth of Witworth's purpose; it was hard to see beyond the lie in the magic.

I drove on.

The Manor was surrounded by forest, ancient oaks and beech. Ash and birch. Thick ferns underfoot were a playground. The few fond memories of the place were in its nature.

As the narrow road rounded, my headlights caught two moving figures darting into the trees.

My guilt welled; I knew who they were.

Turning off the headlights, I parked and walked out into the woods. "I know you're there, it's Adaline."

The two witches came out. One willowy and fair, the other broad and dark.

"Adaline? Really?" She stepped forward, dagger in hand. She was a woman now, but I remembered Eguono as an angry teen. Her coarse hair was cropped short, and she was bundled in a thick coat.

"Yes. I've been summoned."

Her arm dropped and mouth went lax. The other wept softly.

"Why are you out here?" My glance darted to their bags.

"They want to put her in the Door." Eguono's soft Nigerian accent belied the horror of her words.

Yoane shivered, her tears falling softly.

Eguono stepped closer and spoke quietly. "Yoane is a well-witch but couldn't master the power."

"She's only forty. It can take decades to manage it."

Eguono shook her head. "It gets worse. She saw something. She cast at the brook in the woods. They made her go her every day, and I guarded her. It took from her every time."

As she spoke, I looked at Yoane. Her huge watery eyes were vacant, and I ached.

"She drew a well, but it was wrong. It was darkness, and there was only death and fire."

Yoane blinked and looked at me. "She has come."

Eguono went on in a rushed whisper. "They made her tell them and said it was time for her to go through the Door and meet our god, that her place had been ordained. They don't even pretend anymore. Something has changed. They are bold."

"And you're running away?"

"She came here for sanctuary, like most of us. We all believed that's what this place was."

She had no idea that their reasons for sanctuary were orchestrated, some of which were at my doing.

I felt sick. The off-ness of the past week whirled, and the impulsive little shadow which dwelt in me opened an eye.

"Then hurry. Here." From my pocket, I pulled out a wedge of cash. "You can glamour?"

Eguono nodded and took the cash.

"Then do it. Take a train to London. Go to the Well Guardian. He will help you."

"We can't." She looked aghast.

"You must. The Guardian is not who you think. Everything this place tells you is a lie and a glamour. Do you understand?"

She nodded, and Yoane put an icy hand on my face. "I saw you in the well." Her teeth chattered, and I wondered how much longer she'd survive. "You were the fire."

"Go."

They hurried into the woods and vanished.

I drove on. Flashes of my mother's admonishments and fear at my power ran through my mind. Our kind doesn't develop power so young. I knew I was an exception and what that meant. Nothing about it was good.

I was a particularly dangerous cog.

THE SWEETEST LIES CARRY OUR GHOSTS

Witworth Manor stood for three hundred years. It took its name from the horror in its foundations. There wasn't much I was afraid of, but I was of the Manor.

The familiar walls welcomed me in, and I tasted the glamour as it whispered to me. It's a strange power I never mastered. My only skill in bending reality was not being seen, and even then, it was spotty.

The ability to control the appearance of places and bodies would have been useful in my work.

I swallowed the disdain in my gullet for the pristine history of the place. It was steeped in mystery and righteous servitude for the greater good. It was a load of shit. The cloying smell of lilies from the orangery made my eyes water.

"Well. There you are." Lady Witworth stood in the great panelled hall and was as old as the manor with her artful white hair coiled on her head. She leant on a cane with her black eyes narrowed.

"She's definitely dead."

"You saw her?" The pert, warbling tone echoed.

"Yes. I saw her. Identified the body. I saw the house. Nothing there." The itch in my mind of what was off sunk in. The cottage where I'd lived had not been lived in. I put that thought aside.

"Good. As it should be." Lady Witworth tapped along the floor, her cane clinking loudly. I followed. In the library, panelled and filled with the scent of books and dust, the others waited. This was the only room I liked.

"We're ready." Witworth laughed, taking a small sherry waiting for her. I hoped it had arsenic in it, though I knew it probably wouldn't kill her, unfortunately. The gangling horrors that made up the Council were already waiting, lounging on leather couches and tall mahogany chairs and their chatter almost sounded happy.

The Council was made up of twelve of some of the oldest witches and separate to our government of Court. The corruption in the Council was complete. They'd fallen one by one over the centuries to the evil they were sworn to defend us against. They'd survived our most brutal war, but I wondered who'd actually won.

I bowed my head before looking up. Above the large, old stone fireplace, hung a painting. A woman, classically depicted in flowing white robes with a tit out, stood atop a mountain of skulls. The Bringer. I didn't hold with prophecy or chosen ones. It was a running joke as far as I was concerned. The Bringer, apparently, was to lead the Great Death. No-one really bought into it, seeing as it had been made up some time in the 1920s.

Blinking, and feeling old, I turned from the fireplace and poured myself a whisky. "What happens now?"

"We need there to be no impediments." Lady W's smug tone grated as I drank.

"Apparently mother had a solicitor and an insurance policy, and I'm being investigated."

"That might be an issue, do we know who it is?" Grant, the eldest other than Witworth herself, had suspicion in his voice. He hated me ever since I stabbed him in the groin for feeling me up when I was younger. I smiled at the memory of his scream and drained the glass.

Lady W shushed them as they murmured. They were rarely all in the same place at the same time and the congregated monsters obeyed.

"What next?" I knew what they'd say. I'd known it when the council secretary called to tell me my mother was dead.

"You're special, Adaline. An important part of our lives and future. This place is a family. Your aunt brought you to us and saved you from your mother. We've nurtured and loved you. Now it's time to repay us and do your duty." Lady W tapped her cane, and my aunt Matilda came in. My mother had no actual sister, and they looked nothing alike. Her watery eyes were cast down, and she looked frail and unkempt. Another prisoner of this place.

I hadn't seen her in a decade, but I didn't move. Fear had consumed my childhood, but I'd never understood it until I met Matilda.

"Tell us about the man." Lady W smirked at me as I stared at Matilda.

I didn't want to give them his name. "Tell me about my mother."

Matilda looked up. "Your mother was one of us. When she was of age, as you are now, she was asked to align, and you were the result."

"My mother was significantly older than me when she went through the Door. Most witches are still honing their powers at my age."

"But you are not other witches. You are more than a child of the Door. You hide it and think we don't know. Do you truly understand what you are?"

I took a step back, bile filling my throat.

"Your mother ran away, using her magic, and hid you away from us. She was terrified of you. So we thought it was best you come here where you belong."

Sweat beaded on my back, and hot ice ran in my blood. To align furthered the Council's power and connection to the Door. A terrible thing that destroyed my mother, that created me, and corrupted the fabric of our natures. I'd expected my turn since I was a child, but to hear it said upended my control.

Pale and hidden from the eyes of others, a figure appeared at my side. Percival Witworth had been my companion since I arrived. Not many saw the dead, and he was careful to whom he revealed himself.

"Well." He leant his phantom weight on a hip and tilted his head. "I think it's time to leave." Long black hair, breeches and shirt, but all translucent and indistinct. A seventeenth-century fuckboi. "You must leave now, or they'll be no escape, and you'll become your mother or worse."

I took a deep breath. Everything I needed was in my car, but there were too many people between me and the exit.

"In fact, the best thing you can do is burn this place to the ground. They think you're one of them. They believe they've done enough for your complicity." He shimmered. "We talked of this. It is time. You know what will happen to you."

I did. In the dark, blood-soaked bowels of the Manor, where poorly fitted pipes and rot bloomed, and where no glamour could touch, my trap waited for me. A fear so dark that my mother was no longer the woman I'd seen in a few photos, but a traumatised witch who was terrified of the monster she created. Closing my eyes, I saw myself surrounded by evil, by the coming storm, and I rose from the filth. I would never bow to the fate ordained to me by Witworth and its master on the other side. Yoane had said it. I wonder if they knew she was gone yet.

My mind emptied. From a dark recess, my silent companion, so often quelled and silent, took form. It filled my body and took my control. I never let it out or used its terrifying power. I'd kept it so secret that no-one had any thought as to what I was. Its power seeped through, and it was that which my mother feared, not me. The key to my survival had been to give them enough to not suspect.

They thought I was as gullible as any weak, human mortal. As if I didn't know. As if my power wasn't strong enough to fight back. As if I wasn't a cold monster made.

Pouring another drink with my back turned, the Council chatted among themselves. They whispered of my sacrifice, of how none had come back from the Door in years, and it was never happy. The end was coming. I was their chosen Bringer.

Fuck that.

My mother had prepared me well, and nobody knew. I kept that secret for nearly twenty years. Not as simple as good, bad and right or wrong. It was about survival. I glanced at Percival, who flickered and waited in a corner for me.

I cracked my neck and murmured into my glass. The power hummed through the amber liquid and my heart. A prickling in my throat, brain and limbs. It intensified, hot and painful, the dark pressure in the void of my soul and weighted heart bloomed like the alcohol in my belly. I felt the spark ignite, a warm spike of power. Delicious.

A screaming, pitchy wail pierced the room, and it came from no person there. The house itself, or the Door, screeched out an alarm of danger and attack. The Council murmured their disbelief. The vapid, arrogant creatures thought no-one would challenge them. Before they realised their danger, I made my getaway. In through a hidden panel next to the drinks table, I hurried. Percival Witworth led the way, and we navigated the draughty, pitch-black servant passages. Dark and musty, they were frigid and narrow, rough brick bones of the house, full of dust and webs, but Percival glowed with ethereal light and led me to a secret, and I think even Lady W had forgotten it.

More than a priest hole, it was a way out. Hidden at a corner of one of the secret ways, there was a flat gap near the floor just big enough to crawl through. I squeezed down into it, shuffling along on my elbows and knees.

Spiders and cobwebs covered every inch of the rough stone and dead space. Pinching my mouth closed, I went quickly while they tickled me, catching my hair and squashing under my hands. The tunnel was long, and my thighs screamed as I crawled. Eventually, I came to an end and pushed up a tight brick opening filled with mulching leaves.

It came out at the edge of the drive. Originally, it had exited in the surrounding ancient woods as a hidden escape but long forgotten, it was now concealed under the gravel drive. I always parked right by it.

I brushed the dirt, webs and spiders off me, keeping low.

Smoke found its way out, and the glamour flickered out. The house was blackened and warped, rot and decay oozed heat and death. The great doors opened, others spilling out in their pyjamas screaming in horror and shock.

I fished for my keys, but appearing before me, Matilda grabbed my wrist, pushing us against my car.

"Don't."

"I'm not doing it. I will not be a pawn of evil." I struggled.

Percival stood with me in silence.

"We're not evil."

I fell dead-weight, catching her off guard and threw her back. She landed with a thud.

"But you're not good. You're not even my real fucking aunt." I sneered and put my hand over her mouth as I pinned her down. "Listen. You weren't my saviour. I always knew the truth. I'm not stepping through that fucking door."

I pinned her arms with my knees, and with one free hand, I rooted in my pocket, while she struggled under me in a frenzy. A small vial, warm to the touch, sparkled in the orange light as I showed it to her.

Her eyes went wide, and she struggled more.

I pressed down harder. "In the old days, they hanged us. Crushed our bodies or drowned us. Mortal humans and our kind alike. Most of the time, they were wrong and innocent people were murdered. Do you know who Lady Witworth really is?"

Matilda went still.

"She orchestrated much of the death to protect that thing in the cellar. This place is built on the death of mortals and witches alike. She went against our purpose. We were here to protect against the darkness." I leant down close to Matilda. "She was seduced by the horror and power of the evil on the other side of the glass. You do her bidding because that's what you're conditioned to do. Her rules are bullshit. The glamour can't hold anymore."

The ruin of the house was engulfed in flame, windows blew out and fire roared, the heat from it licked my skin, and I was inwardly sated. Smoke filled the air, billowing out from the chimneys and windows, flames licking the walls. The ground shuddered and cracked. The tension in the brick itself vibrated. I threw my head back with her pinned under me. I willed more fire, I bent the flame, until the brick glowed, and my skin burnt.

The crowd of less than twenty scattered down the drive, but we were hidden in darkness. The strangled cry from the evil still screamed in the fire. I focused on the Door. I saw it pulse in my mind. Matilda was screaming as her cheek blistered.

"You know, I might be the coming death, but not for humans. For you." My voice became bent and ugly, and my body twitched as if I had no control over it. It was the other part of me, glorying in getting to play.

The shadow laughed in my heart and wanted to dance in the flames.

I took my hand from her face, and as she gasped, I shoved the vial in and clamped her jaw shut. The poison took her quickly. The glass crunched in her mouth and body convulsed. The smell of evil lessened. I gave her no thought or care; she'd given me none. My internal shadow receded at the smell of the potion, and as fast as I could, I picked up my keys, and started my car, peeling out of the drive, spewing up gravel as I went.

The handful of young ones sheltered by the elders looked on, confused. Esher, Lady W's right hand, ran after me, and behind her, I saw the tiny pale figure of Percival fade. It only occurred to me that with the death of the house, I'd never see him again.

I shut down the regret and pain, gripping the wheel and drove.

WHAT TO SAY WHEN THE TONGUE IS SPLIT

stank of fire. The service station I stopped at was deserted other than for a lone lorry driver tucking into a full English breakfast.

I didn't remember the drive or anything much, other than I'd done it. Hollow sadness welled as I perched in grating strip light and tacky utility. It was two in the morning, and I hugged my tea tight. I felt nothing, staring until my vision doubled.

The man a few tables over glanced at me as he finished the last of his greasy food and wiped his mouth, but my bitch face must have been on point. He looked away.

I wondered what he saw. Who he saw. Tallish. Dark red hair. Nearly black eyes. Strong cheekbones. The approximation of a person. Bitch. Witch. Victim?

I sighed. I thought of Mr Church, oddly. In my pocket, I found his battered card but didn't remember him giving it to me. I turned it over and put it on the table. Black card, gold ink. Something off about it. Familiar. I smelt it, and it wasn't human; it smelt different. My mouth salivated at the scent but at the impulse to lick it, I put it down, keeping my finger on it.

Church would learn about Witworth and me. Possibly other things. I needed to know who he was and how much reach he had. My thoughts wandered back to the cottage. I almost wished I'd summoned her, her name on my tongue and dead body in the morgue. I absently ran my hand over the card. Something, something on the tip of thought and I couldn't reach it. The shadow was too present and restless.

I fished in my pocket, and another little vial warmed in my hands. It was clear but for a pale blue light that ran through it. I took it in one, and I calmed, my mind clear and quiet.

My phone screen had cracked in my escape, but it was still usable. I put the company name in the search. Church and Associates Investigative and Protective Services brought up a fair few results. Not the niftiest of titles.

A shadow interrupted my research, and the truck driver stood in front of me.

I didn't look up, though I saw. "I wouldn't if I were you."

He sat opposite.

"What did I just say?" I projected my voice and a group of drunk people that disembarked from a coach outside came in. They all heard. "Leave me alone. Stop harassing me."

He shook his head when I looked at him. "I knew Estelle."

All my blood pooled into my feet. "Do not say her name."

"Your mother was not who you think."

I braced. "And who do you think I assume her to be? And who are you for that matter?"

Soft warmth lay in his pale grey eyes as he eased down into the seat opposite. "I've been watching you for some time, making sure nothing happened to you, and observing the Council, but now she's gone..." He pinched his mouth and finished the mug of the tea he'd brought over. "Not everyone falls into the 'ruin humanity' camp. Some of us still work for the greater good. You are part of that. Not everyone abandoned you to Witworth. There have been shifts. Lost ones found. Pockets of evil conquered. But you. You're the one."

"Ugh, not this." I rubbed my forehead.

"Not some destined The One bollocks they spout off about. They do it to make young ones feel important. It's propaganda. But you brought Witworth to its knees. None of us has been able to do that. Listen, I know that place, what it pretends to be and what it really is."

"What do you think it is?"

"Your mother, along with a number of others, myself included, were working for the Court. We were sent to investigate Witworth Council."

Well, that I didn't know. He had my attention and saw it.

I pocketed my phone and the card and sat back. "Go on."

"My father fought in the Middle War. He was old when it began. He'd tell me about history. When Shakespeare was alive. I was born in 1810. My father told me about the war. Sir Percival quelled the Door at Witworth and built the Manor right in the middle of a century-long war. It became a base for us to learn and fight. Percy was my father's friend and hero. He even took its name as a way to claim his duty when he married Johanna. Think about it like this, the Council used their power to create the glamour there in order to hide the Door, but it's deep rooted and widespread. They were originally a refuge after the middle war ended, gathering stray witches, and outwardly that's what they do." He gave me a pointed look. "But their purpose was corrupted over the years, seeking to open it fully."

"I helped them. Found lost witches and gave them sanctuary." That was my shame. My place as a ticking cog.

"They built over the Door to contain and learn from it. In hindsight, it wasn't a good idea, but Percival was extraordinary. He fought like few I ever knew of. A master of demons and a visionary. He could've been King Elect of Court but took on the duty of Guardian. Johanna seemed everything good and pure and stood at his side in the fight. She glamoured us all, it's her true skill. Percival was Door Guardian but was lost to its horror. We suspect by Johanna's hand, but we were never sure."

I didn't say anything.

"There were whispers for decades after Percival vanished, but in the 1900s, our Queen Elect, Musa, set up our unit to find out what happened to Percival and if the Manor was secure because she could get no answers. Johanna glamoured herself, the place, every person who went there. Your mother led the covert unit."

I leant forward with my hands flat on the warm laminated table. "Witworth took her in, found out she was a spy and fed her to the Door."

"And you are the result." His gaze was focused and hopeful, but fear sat behind it, and he focused on my hands.

"What do you want?" I put them in my pockets.

"Join us."

Of course, my power would go a long way to help them. I'm the creature you employ to do the dirty shit. "Why didn't my mother go back to you lot?"

"She was afraid for you. Exposing your power was too dangerous. She kept in touch with me, and used a glamour to hide you, though it wasn't a skill for her."

No, it seemed not.

I drank my tea. "Do you know what I really am? A product of evil. There is no denying it. I killed Matilda and put others at risk. What you ask is all out war. We barely survived that last one."

"This isn't war, Adaline," he leant forward, "this is the end. It's already here. All we can do now is resist. There is no-one better, plus, how long do you think you can go alone?" He turned his head away as though listening for a few seconds and when he turned back, he spoke in a low rushed tone. "You remember Len?"

"Yes."

"He can help you."

I tapped the table with my finger. The light hurt my eyes. "How?"

"He works for the Court. He can shelter you. You should go." His warmth evaporated.

Unsure if it was hunters or Witworth on my heels, I left.

I was crossing the car park when, lights flickered.

"Adaline."

I turned as I opened the car door.

"Trust the church."

"What?"

"I dreamt of you. Witworth burned, and you were in a church. Safest place."

I scowled with a nod and drove, knowing where I was heading. It was a bad idea, but I went to Church, only it wasn't the kind of church my new friend was thinking of.

Behind me, I saw him turn away and vanish before the car park lights went out completely.

△ △ △

Back in the town where Mr Church worked, on a hilly street about an hour from my mother's house, I mapped the distances in my mind, turning a cigarette over in my hand. Sharp angles and narrow roads encroached by bland modernity were shrouded in pre-dawn light. I watched a building as the sun rose.

I saw him. Same coat and suit. Mr Church made his way to it, pausing. I willed myself to be seen by him, and he scowled.

It started raining again. I murmured, putting the unlit cigarette back in the pack and pushed off the wall I'd been leaning on and crossed the road.

It was early, and the traffic hadn't yet started to clog the place. It was a peaceful dawn. My favourite time of day.

Mr Church sighed deeply, eyeing me with suspicion. It was kind of adorable. For a mortal.

"Come on." He led the way in. The old building was cold, a higgledy-piggledy office conversion. He made us coffee.

He sniffed at me as we went in. I looked around the office while he made us a drink. I sat at his desk when set the mugs down before hanging up his coat.

"Tell me, why do you smell of a fire?"

"I started one."

He pressed his thumbs to his forehead and deep-breathed. "Of course."

I grimaced. "I need to know what you know. What are the caveats? Specifics."

He sipped his coffee, turned on his computer and unlocked a drawer. "All right. Let's play this game. Here." He tossed down a brown folder and in it was my mother's will. "Est-"

"Don't say her name."

"Your mother," he said slowly, drawing it out with his gaze set on me, "was convinced you were evil. I knew she was orphaned with her sister and they lived in a home. The purpose of which is pretty vague, a private institution that was some sort of retreat, school, hospital, who knows? The same institution you lived in for a time."

I didn't look at him. All public record and none of it true.

"It's a notoriously difficult place to contact. People just seem to fade from record. Your aunt, for example, has no work record. She doesn't claim anything. Not on the electoral roll, never married, nothing. No bank records, no car, just... nothing."

He waited for me to speak. I didn't.

"As far as caveats go, that's simple enough. I'm to investigate whether you have any connection to the death of your mother. The insurance will only pay if no suspicion falls on you for any crime or wrongdoing."

"You're to decide that?"

"No, I seek facts only. It's up to the solicitor or police. Seeing as you're a confessed arsonist." He shrugged before sitting forward and resting his arms on the desk. "I've been doing this a long time, and I get a feel for people. You didn't kill her. I think you're as invested in knowing the truth as I am."

"Did you rehearse that little skit?"

He grinned. It spread across his face and was lovely.

I read the will. The house and contents were mine, specifically the doctors' bag. I set it down, leaning back in my chair, and briefly flicked through the insurance policy. The office was cold, and I put my hands back in my pockets when I was done. "I didn't know what I looked like for years. She never kept mirrors in the house, she said they held too much power. She kept the windows grimy and smeared them with weird mud. She said it was so that evil couldn't look at me.

"I thought it was more so I couldn't look at my face. Do you believe in good and evil, Mr Church?"

He didn't answer for a time and drank his coffee in silence. "Not too far from here, there's a cottage. The people who lived in it were strange. They lived long lives, and the history goes back hundreds of years. To witches. There are so many local legends about that place. Ghosts and haunted hills.

"There's one story about a mirror. It was said the mirror was a portal to a prison, and it's where witches would put demons. There are all sorts of mirrored portals and strange doors that connect a network of places no good person wishes to go. They're called Mirrorwells. These portals have inspired cults and fanatics. Whole religions and cultures spawned from the horror going back centuries, most of which were distorted, or the origins forgotten.

They rise and fall. Some powerful, some merely strange. But all have the same thing. Good and evil forces and a way to travel through them."

I didn't breathe. "And you think my mother believed this?"

"Oh, she did. It's as much as I know about her."

"Do you believe them?"

He didn't answer but twitched a smile. "So you burnt Witworth to the ground last night."

I pulled my hands out my pockets and held my mug.

"It collapsed in on itself. It's too hot to go in yet. Took all night to put out. You look relieved. What's going on?" When Church spoke, it was easy to listen. I didn't react to humans. They had their uses, sex mostly, but he was... compelling. Untainted.

I shook my head. "You don't want involvement in this."

"Well, you say that, but you came to me, and those words aren't exactly dissuasive."

Ignoring him, I checked the news on my phone. Witworth was there top of the page, camera footage from a helicopter, flames blazing high.

Three people missing, one body found.

"Mr Church, there are hungry things in the world. Not animals necessarily, but some things which eat. They leave bones and dust and mystery. Witworth is one of those things. It'd be wiser to leave it be."

"I'm being paid to investigate for a solicitor and insurance company, the death of your mother. The pay-out is two million."

Tilting my head, I couldn't make sense of it, it wasn't something she'd risk. "How could she afford a policy like that?"

"The house was paid for, there was no money in the bank, but the policy and bills were always on time and paid in full."

Standing, I buttoned up my coat. "Mr Church, you should be careful, these people are dangerous, so don't go chasing the ghosts of Witworth. They bite."

"That's a blatant lure. Wait." He pursed his lips, wrestling with something.

"Say it."

He laughed and rounded the desk. "You know how once you say a thing, there's no unsaying it. This is ridiculous."

Facing him in front of the window, the day was suddenly bright. I stared at the sun on brick behind him. A clock ticked slowly, time keeling off to the side. There was something gentle and honest about him, but I didn't trust it.

He frowned.

"Tell me what you're afraid to say."

"Your mother believed in demons and witches and things in the dark. She thought the Mirrorwell was real and tried to steal it, by which I mean she went to the cottage I told you about and broke in. Two weeks later, she was dead."

I had to face this. Make choices. Percival was gone. Life as I knew it had ended. I almost heard mother say trust him. He was so compelling. I swallowed all the saliva that filled my mouth and fixed on his lips. The sweet lure of him felt like a trap, but the man at the service station was wrong; I couldn't trust him. The room turned slowly, and against the warning in my mind, I went on.

"Do you know what the true systems of magic are?"

He waited, patient and silent as he had done at the house, accepting and trusting. Too innocent.

"Three systems. One is mortal witchcraft, always practised throughout humanity in some capacity. There are two hidden systems. Immortal magic from the existence of reality and the third is the unworldly. Not of our reality or realms. Demons."

I balled my fist in my pocket, waiting for him to laugh, but Church didn't move and met my gaze.

Weighing up the truth, I bit the inside of my lip, unable to not say it. "I'm from the second group, technically. We had one task set to us. Our existence was a response to the threat of the evil that came through portals. The Doors. There were those that fell to the seduction on the other side of these unnatural pathways."

Shaking his head, he screwed up his face. "I don't understand..."

This moment was wrong. "These are not mortal matters, stay away. Goodbye, Mr Church."

GUARDIAN, GUARDIAN, PROTECT ME FROM THE DARK

That had been a terrible mistake. My hands shook. I felt him follow, and part of me wanted to bring him to me and protect him. I resisted and left. That impulse was not of me, I felt no such things for humans.

As I hurried back to my car, I saw a shadow. I smelt the corruption in the air and knew I had to get away. Witworth or hunters again, hard to tell the difference anymore, but I needed to draw them away from the mortal. The need to protect him stuttered my heart, and I steeled myself against it.

My next move would be key. I didn't want to go to Len because trusting the Court wasn't an instinct I possessed, though Len had once been one of my only friends. I didn't want to lead danger to the Court either. Tapping the wheel as I eased into traffic, I thought about Yoane and her vision. I decided to go the Well Guardian and headed north.

Things were about to get weird. I hated weird.

The Well Guardian occupied a space and time not in our reality. It was a form of glamour, but powerful and intense, and unlike our magic. It came from somewhere else.

The ways to the Well Guardian changed around. I had to taste it. The most common was via an old library in London, but the secret, hidden road I sought was barely used. I caught the familiar scent of my old friend and his strange life after a few hours of travelling in a vague direction. I filled up with petrol once I found it, determined not to think of Mr Church, and went in to pay and grab food.

The attendant behind the counter had a wet cough and a pale face. I eyed him, beads of sweat gathered in his hairline, and a flush appeared every time he coughed. I bought some hand sanitiser with a sense of foreboding.

I headed on, gaining physical and spiritual distance from Witworth, Mr Church and my mother. I passed out of all human sight onto hidden roads. I moved out of the mortal world. The road I drove along was rocky and uneven and marked by tall stones carved with odd symbols I didn't recognise. Incantations I could almost hear were whispered in the air, though the language was alien. I was surrounded by a valley of grey stone and an unearthly pink sky loomed when I neared.

The place wasn't real and yet was truth.

Once a pilgrimage for all witches, it was forgotten and lay barren and desolate.

A grey building, known as Rhere's temple —he always said it was an echo of home — was a tall, peaked triangle of smooth stone with no visible windows. It called to me as I parked, my skin glowing in the pink light, and from an unseen door a figure appeared. He was more than seven-foot-tall with black hair and bone-white skin, and his eyes were the night sky. He terrified me and was a true friend, and he greeted me as any witch might.

He was not a witch, nor a human. Rhere. That wasn't his full name, he told me once over vodka when we were drunk, but it was too guttural, and he fell off the bench laughing at me trying to say it.

"I have been waiting." A streak of prismed light flickered over his skin from within, and it shimmered from white to bronze and back again.

"Old friend."

"Come. There are others." His sharp accent bent the vowels. The closest I thought it sounded like was maybe Icelandic, or Finnish, but then he'd slip into languages that sounded alien to me, and modern English confused him.

I asked him once where he came from, and he wept. A dead world, he said, and we toasted a god. A sun eater he called him, his father.

Around the huge central firepit, others sat and ate. In the darkened recesses were bunks and cupboards, stacks of books and gifts brought to him as offerings. Nothing aged or changed, and no dust settled.

"The Court came here not three weeks past, and the Queen Elect herself sat at my hearth and ate with me in abundance. And now you join me. You sent these?" He gestured to Eguono and Yoane.

I laughed and put my hand over my heart. "I did, though I bring you no gifts, except..." I pulled out a bag of sweets.

Taking them, he ate one and grinned. He tilted his head. "I have been alone for many years, waiting, and now all seems to want my hospitality." He gave me a knowing look, and I was trapped in the glittering depth of his eyes. "What is it? You grieve so."

Tears burnt. "My mother died."

He bowed his head cupped his hands into a ball, murmuring a prayer.

I waited with bowed head until he was finished. "I need answers, but I don't know the questions, and can we not talk in riddles."

He smiled, so warm and odd. "First we eat and drink."

I sat by Yoane who had colour in her face again, and the hard, vacant look in her eyes from when I saw her before had dimmed. She touched my hand. "Thank you."

I squeezed hers in return. "I burnt Witworth."

Everyone stilled, even the fire seemed to hold its breath. I looked into the deep flames of an old fire that had burnt without cease for thousands of years. "I lit no match, I let my shadow run free and destroyed it."

"But not the Door." Yoane trembled.

I looked at Rhere's horrified face. "No, no witch can."

"Hmm." He poured the drinks.

I took the glass and toasted the fire and company and drank, as was custom, and ate the warm herbed bread. Nothing tasted so good right then, and I couldn't remember the last time I ate in company and safety. For a singular second, I remembered nothing at all, and I wanted to sing.

"There was a time when all witches came to me. It was rite. I blessed them with my blood and showed them the well, and then I told them their fate and destiny. They understood their history and purpose. Now I am relic and watch television." He shrugged one shoulder before taking a shot and refilling the glasses. "You have come to see it."

Yoane and Eguono fell quiet and abruptly said goodnight, retiring to the bunks.

I understood their reluctance. "No."

"You always lie to yourself."

"The truth isn't safe."

"Ha!" He drank again. He stared for a moment. "What are you afraid of?"

"My part. That it's not a lie, and I am..."

"Who is destined?" he sneered. "There are twelve children of the Door. The vision is known and old but kept secret. For it cannot be spoken of. You are the youngest surviving that is known. Its children will die, and the Door will open. It is said. Also, it is bullshit."

"There are twelve of us. I've seen the records." I stared into my glass before drinking.

"Then it is not bullshit." Rhere seemed to be deciding if it was a question or answer, and then turned to the fire.

When he didn't speak, I filled the quiet. "It is and it isn't. There are prophecies upon prophecies. All shrouded in some mystery of which cannot be spoken. I've been part or witness to many, and they all failed. Every one. Some witch had the gift of visions and saw some version of reality. That's it."

"Reality? Young one, what do you know of it?" His firm voice was little more than a hiss. "Infinite walls separate all time. My reality is of star gods and serpent kings. There's another in which you didn't ever reach Witworth, and your mother sent you to me as I asked her to. She said it was too dangerous. How was that place ever safe for you, Door Child?" He took a shot.

We were silent, and I let that turn over.

"Others will come. Pilgrimage will begin." He kept too still.

"There are so many lies, it's hard to put it all in order. Maybe the hunters are right and we're all evil."

He turned his mouth down. "In my world they were called priests. At first in this place they called themselves the same. I was here before the Doors were summoned. I remember the tumult when they were. I felt it. But then, I was god, a serpent of another reality, brought into death and chaos."

I squinted. "How drunk are you?"

"Always, and very. So would you be. I have waited for it to wake, to be over. The end is always chasing the living. Death wins. I have seen worlds brought to bone and dust, and yours will be next. I am so old, and you're all so young."

The sorrow in his voice hurt my heart.

"I remember coming here for the first time. I came with Len when we left Witworth. You helped him, and we got really drunk."

"No, you came with your mother when you were baby. I held and blessed you in the dark. I felt your strength even then. But strength doesn't mean prophecy is real or that you'll have ability. All different things. That time with Len, I hoped you'd stay, but you went back."

"I'm a coward. If I could change anything, it would be that."

We were silent for a time. I moved the fire with my will, curling the flame to and fro. There was a density to it, a resistance, like playing with a kitten. Mother never let me play, and any casual use was dangerous but after the release of burning the Manor down, I was uncorked. I smirked at its movement.

"I have lived for years incalculable. I've been on this planet in this reality since men were nomads and there were no cities. I have seen everything. No witch has ever mastered fire."

"None had the power?"

"That is not what I said. It eats them. More witches perish from their power than anyone will tell you. Lesser witches survive. Come, let's go to the well, and you will know." He knocked back a drink and strode out.

I followed. I was sure he homebrewed that stuff because it knocked a punch. I swayed. I'd been under his roof a dozen times. Once, I was so beaten from a fight with a pack of hunters, he'd tended me when I made it there. He'd been afraid of me then. I never asked why.

He held out an unlit torch, and I lit it. He smiled as he turned to me for a second and we descended a spiral stone stairway. It felt like we were going up at the same time as going down. At the bottom, I tried to look up, too dizzy to do it, and all turned. I was unsure if it was the vodka or magic.

"It'll pass." The sound echoed.

The circle we stood in had doors off it with words carved above each triangular doorway. A smooth black glass underfoot circled a black octagon that rose about a foot off the floor.

"In my world, there were great temples like this. They rose into the sky for the dead god who was our father. The great fallen sun eater, a king, he was death come to form. I am his son."

Rhere set the torch in a sconce and cupped his hands to his face. "My father, receive this witch."

My skin goosed, and I stepped forward. In the raised glass altar was the well, a liquid shimmered, but it was not water, it was black. It sparkled like the night sky and Rhere's eyes.

"What is it?" I knew that horror lived within in it, and I grew cold.

"Death. It is like all doors. The idea is a constant, but its execution is a matter of physics. This power in this well is that of a true god, born in creation, it devoured time and stars, and fell in love and sacrificed itself to mortality. Its remains are a conduit through all reality and time. My kind are scattered through it. The Lost Sons of the Serpent God." His voice echoed through my bones, and heat shimmered in me, making me steam in the frigid air.

My shadow awakened.

He expelled a breath. "There, I feel what you have suppressed."

The floor keeled, and I turned over. His voiced slowed and deepened.

"You are not what you think. Your end is coming as all will fall." He seemed to grow, towering, his skin a deep purple, then bronze, then sparkling white. All colour and depth, all time and knowledge. I saw who he was.

Rhere was gone. "The end has begun, Witworth has broken, but that is not the danger now. You are. They will come."

He flickered out of reality, and I was drawn to the altar with everything warping around me.

"It kills all but the strongest, it devours mortals yet demands no sacrifice. That which dwells beyond the Doors wants to eat your reality, and their prisons fail now with the coming of one."

The torch went out.

DARK REALITY AND ITS POISON

There was only the sound of my breath, and then hot arms around me. I opened my eyes to Rhere smiling strangely. I struggled but he shushed, and the galaxy in his gaze calmed me.

"Most become catatonic when they see. What did you see?"

"You, but not you."

"My father appeared? How interesting."

"Not really."

He grinned as I stood up. We were still at the altar.

"So this is another kind of Door."

He made a noise. "For my kind. There is only me left that I know of. I'm a dragon, you know."

I did a double take.

"It's been many years, it's no longer safe to show my true form. My time is at an end. The war that is here will leave no room for me. I shall descend and pray for death. My father will welcome me home, but first, I will help you." He nodded firmly.

We went back up, but it was hard to look away. It whispered to me, calling me back. I halted. "It wants me."

"You hear it? I hear it. We have long conversations."

"It wants to..."

"Enter you. Yes, yes, that never goes well."

I turned and went back down.

"Adaline." He boomed, and I halted. Heat kindled. "No."

It was a roar, and he put his arms around me. I convulsed, fire bursting from me, throwing him back, singed.

"It will kill you, do not give in. You will only give your demon strength over you. You will lose."

My hand stretched out; skin glowing. A vein of black tar rippled up from the font.

"You will lose yourself."

I saw my mother pacing on the deck. The mould on the ceiling. A bird cawing from a fence, my mother's hair, her scent of flowers, her voice singing. The taste of Palma Violets.

"This is not your path."

"Why does it want me?" My voice wasn't mine.

"Power. The creatures, the demons need power. A vessel to survive this reality. I should have never brought you here."

It was his fear that did it. Rhere was my friend. A strange, frightening presence, but kindness softened his danger, and now he feared me.

"Help me."

He grunted and muttered something. His bones cracked, and he looked denser, grimmer, and moved with unnatural speed. All the while, I moved in slow motion, unattached to my body. It moved vapour-like; my physical body ungainly and strange. The curl of tar sparkled like a clear night. I heard my mother crying, and with a roar, just as it touched my outstretched hand, I was snatched away.

The iron grip pinched me, and I screamed, descending into a hiss, and flame curled over my lips. Rhere covered my mouth and leapt upward, staring deep into my eyes. I spaced out with a sweet sense of calm.

He dropped me at the top of the stairs, his clothes smoking as he patted them. "That's a thing that just happened and I thought I'd seen everything."

I knew a truth; one I hadn't looked for. Mother was right.

I took a vial from my pocket. The shadow I'd suppressed was not just power. It was not me compartmentalising trauma and power in order to survive. It was infinitely more.

"How have you lived with it?"

I sank to my knees. "Mother prepared me well." I held up the vial. "Her gift was potions."

I knocked it back and the danger passed.

"You should take a bath." He nodded and pointed to the room and I went in. My holdall was already set inside. He locked it behind me. Fair enough.

I ran cold water into the stone tub, and heated it with my hand, circling it. My other, the one outstretched to the unfathomable thing that wanted me, I held up, looking at it. Rubbing my thumb and forefinger together, the sensation of it touching me made me shudder. I closed my eyes in the bath, and under my lids I saw myself as a monster, the thing lurking under my skin.

I got out of the bath. A rude mirror hung on a wall, and I glanced at it.

"Mirrors let evil in. They are dangerous." My mother's words. I closed my eyes. It wasn't wholly a lie. They allow the evil to be seen. Being seen gave it power.

I redressed and knocked to be let out.

I shivered, skin goosing when he led me back. Rhere sat at the fire, staring into it. A new witch sat with him, and they spoke in what sounded like Russian.

They looked at me.

"More come." Rhere looked impossibly sad.

"I am sorry, friend."

He nodded and slid a short dagger made of black glass over to me. "Knives should not be given, only sold." He smiled, tapping it.

From my pocket, I pulled out a cherry lollipop.

His brows rose. "Fair exchange." He unwrapped it and smiled, popping into his cheek.

I took the blade, looking at it as the black glass shimmered. I took off my coat, sliding on the holster, and tested pulling it out.

"What is it made of?" I slipped my coat on.

"It is a shard of a door. It will kill you, and any demon that happens your way. So don't touch the blade itself, your skin will melt or freeze. Or something, I don't remember."

The Russian witch spoke to Rhere.

He nodded and translated. "They say the hunters are corrupted by demons. Attacks are increasing across Europe."

I sat next to them and ran my fingers through my hair to dry it near the fire. "Yes. It's been my work for the last year tracking them. Silly plots to kill or take us."

"They recruit in high numbers. More each week."

"Yes."

"You should go, you cannot stay here."

"I know." I looked over at Yoane and Eguono fast asleep together. "I don't know what to do."

"Church." The witch looked at me through narrowed eyes. "I see. Church." She toasted me and drank.

I raised a brow. The bizarre exchange I'd had with Mr Church had paled since being in Rhere's company, and I'd had no plans to revisit him, but it seemed I was going to anyway. There was a light in Church that drew me, and I couldn't let myself be fooled, but now it looked like I was leaving the 'very weird' and settling for 'probably a trap.'

As I readied to leave the one place I thought I'd be safe, regret tugged. I wondered if I'd ever see Rhere again.

At the door, he held my shoulders and hugged me. I was not a hugger, nor he, but I embraced him. He was like warm steel. His massive hand cupped my face, and the stars dimmed in his eyes.

"I grieve for what will be. Who is this Church?"

"I don't know. Too human, but not like anyone. There are things in play here I don't understand."

"Every end begins another, as all things turn. Trust your mother. She was right to be wary."

I tapped his hand and left him, returning to what felt like the right path as I drove away. A path that I hadn't chosen.

The unreality of leaving a strong glamour always threw me. The world looked heavier and dull. Colour insipid and air dirtier.

Two separate witches told me to go to Church. Had seen it. If visions of me were going about, I guess I had to listen.

Rhere seemed like a dream, or nightmare the further away I got, but my fingers still tingled.

I didn't know what day it was, or anything much, and I stopped at a hotel off the motorway as my eyes dropped. The car park was virtually empty. The woman at the desk coughed violently after she gave me my key card.

That sinking feeling came back. I checked the news. Worst flu outbreak on record. Hospitals overwhelmed. Advice was to stay at home.

My heart turned. Traffic had seemed quiet. I thought about the petrol station attendant. Still, the death toll was low so far. The last time there was Door activity there was a world war and Spanish flu.

Something was already happening.

Exhaustion overcame me and I fell asleep working out my next move.

△ △ △

Outside Church's office, in the chilly day, I lit a cigarette and walked a little. I rolled it between my finger and thumb, letting the familiar acrid scent rise bitter around me, though I no longer inhaled. Anxiety bit at me, which was alien, and I wanted to go back to Rhere. My thoughts were chaos.

I'd slept for fifteen hours and ate my own weight in food in the restaurant. There'd not been another soul in there, and hardly any food, but I ate all of it and pocketed as much as I could.

I didn't bother checking out, there was no-one at the desk.

I passed a few people wearing masks, weaving in and out unseen, but it wasn't them I feared, and my mind glanced backwards at the last ten years.

Disconnected, I supposed the things I'd done weren't that bad, but stacking things on top of one another and there's a prism showing something dark. Those cogs turning.

I was too distracted, and something put its arms around me and pinned me against its chest. I couldn't breathe.

The same presence that I felt the other day. It'd been waiting. "Whoa there, girly." It almost sounded human but wasn't.

I stopped struggling, slipping down, and he squeezed.

My throat closed, leaving me unable to speak.

Tensing, I balled energy up into a hot wave and pushed out. It loosened its grip. I did it again with a scream. I whipped around, reached under my coat, pulling the dagger, the green-black glass shimmering, and plunged it into his stomach. I didn't take a human life, I quelled something else that occupied a space where a human once was. These were more common each month. The Russian witch was right. I dragged the blade up until I reached his sternum, the cut smoked and hissed, and he went limp, falling to the ground. I guess it really was realm glass.

I wiped the blade and my hands on his clothes before sheathing it. I listened, but there was nothing but silence. Huffing a humourless laugh, I looked at the dead thing. No blood, just dark goo. They were brazen in the empty streets. They didn't care anymore.

Feeling watched, I looked up to the end of the alleyway. Church stood there.

There was no impulse to fight, no stench of the hatred from him. "Who are you?" he asked breathlessly.

Without answering, I squatted down, sniffing the body. This one was stronger than many. In his pockets, I found a wallet and phone with nothing of interest. The only incoming call was from an unknown number. I tilted my head, and kindled heat, caressing the air with it, and set the thing on fire.

Acrid smoke, like burning tires, went up behind me as I walked to Church, who looked grim and about ten years older. And oddly more attractive.

"Fancy a drink?" I passed him.

He followed. "That... that..."

"Was not human, and I'm wondering how much you know and who you actually work for."

"That's nothing to do with me." Fear sat in his eyes and yet acceptance. He was like a lamb. My heart pinched.

"Are you sure?"

He kept his eyes on the smouldering mess behind me as I passed by. What remained would fade into nothing, its existence erased by natural order.

I halted and turned to Church. "You seem human, but you're not an innocent bystander. Can't be. Last time, who do you work for?"

"No-one," he shouted, throwing his arms out. "I have no idea what any of this means."

"Liar." I walked off, and he followed as I found my car.

"Fine, the solicitor your mother hired occasionally contacts me for jobs, and I investigate things." He spoke in a rush, and I could almost hear his pounding heart in his voice.

"People don't look into us unless they have reason. The question is who are they and what do they want. Drink?"

"Nothing's open, it's morning." He scrubbed his face and hair, mussing it.

"Oh. I've had a very weird... day, two days. When did you seen me last?"

He furrowed his brow and folded his arms. "A week ago."

"Huh. Well, time is relative. Listen, whoever sent that thing wasn't here for me, it was watching you. Two people have told me to trust 'church.' I can't ignore that, but you're clearly not safe and have a role to play. Ready?"

"Not really, but okay."

PRAY FOR PREY AND DEVOUR INNOCENTS

He dithered. "I don't live far."

"Cute, but they'll know where you live." The question was who sent them. My kill was a little pre-emptive. "You know what, let's go to yours."

I drove us, and he glanced at me a few times. "That really happened."

"I've had a really intensely weird time recently, and that one barely registers. Have you been feeling ill at all?"

"No, I'm never ill."

Interesting.

At his flat, modern and stark in the brevity that equated a short mortal life, I looked about.

"I'm kinda hungry." My stomach rumbled.

"I can make eggs."

"Like a chicken?" I picked up a glass paperweight on the sideboard, and next to it was a stack of business cards.

"Scrambled." He watched me intently.

"Sounds good. Where did you get these?" I held one up.

"My employer. The solicitor. He said I should have them and now I have them."

There was something so monumentally wrong about this guy. I shook my head and produced the slightly rumpled one from my pocket. "When did you give me this?"

The corners of his mouth turned down. "I didn't."

"No. That's what I thought, yet here it is."

He took it and turned it over.

My mouth salivated at being near him, and I stepped back. "Bathroom?"

He pointed the way, and I went in. Slipping off my coat, I washed my face and hands; I had demon stink on me. I hadn't noticed being near Church. He was like an air freshener. I scrubbed my arms too.

I glanced at the mirror, the impulse to look away was there as ever, but I didn't. Mother's words in my head. There were two mes. The one that appeared human, and the part of me that lived within, born of horror, it lurked and shifted under my skin, beating on the inside. I flexed my jaw. Rhere had shown me that truth. I'd always thought it was metaphor. Steadying myself, that truth was too real, too huge. It had been so accessible at Rhere's, but in cold mortal physics it was too much.

I looked tired, ready to lose the battle to come. Dark eyes and dark spirit. Being a human never really appealed to me, but I wondered what it would be like as I scrutinised my reflection. Mortal woes and struggles compared to being the harbinger of the end.

Knowledge hovered, things in the dark. I widened my inky black eyes, skin vibrating as my image slipped in and out of reality.

The thing in me punched the glass, casting a thousand shards that hovered. I pulled away from my reflection, finding the glass intact. At the smell of food, I grabbed my coat.

I set it on the breakfast bar and watched him cook.

"You're very attached to that thing." He nodded at my coat. Mid-grey, deep collar, hidden pockets, and woven with a glamour of its own.

"It's warm." He didn't need to know the history or power of it. I tried to wrench my eyes away and look at recent events objectively, yet I kept watching him.

"Who was that thing?"

"Once a human, they're lured with the promise of power and truth. A secret beyond the curtain. It's too tempting for humans. They love those mysteries."

He gave me a wry glance.

"Once they're taken, the human is dead. There are demons, smaller essences of a greater evil. They seep through and take people, or a witch, like me, is captured and... fed to them."

Church looked at the food, then me, and closed his eyes. "Is this like a devil thing?" He scowled and served the soft and buttery eggs.

I was starved but laughed as I settled down to eat. "How trite and cliché." Sipping my tea between mouthfuls, I went on. "It's the nature of humanity to find patterns and assign meaning that fits pre-existing bias, right? Signs and portents blah blah."

Church nodded but frowned. "I thought demons were all to do with hell and the devil. Exorcisms and those things."

"Am I supposed to say something about the discernment of spirits? Or how fervour of the cruel could excite euphoric catharsis of rage and emotion under the guise of possession? I don't care for the trite machinations of human beliefs."

He was drawn and quiet. But I saw how he was rationalising a new reality, and I wondered what patterns he'd find in it. "Go on," he swallowed, hands shaking.

"What I am, and the world I live in has existed for thousands of years and has nothing to do with human religion. All that bullshit goes back to humans wanting to control people. What's pertinent is that in the seventeenth century there was a war of my kind. It raged unseen. Doors were unsealed, and the end began. It was a whole thing. What humans saw was the tail end of it and boy did you run with it. You know how many actual preternatural creatures were caught up in mindless murdering during witch hunts? Five known incidents and they were all orchestrated within the supernatural war. The rest were all human victims."

Church only blinked. "Right. Well."

"Sorry, it annoys me. People give so much credit to a fictional collection of fifth hand information that was incorporated into Christianity."

"No, I got that." He shook his head. "So how do you fit into this?"

"My mother called me a Doomer because I was one of many anointed to bring the end by unsealing the Doors again, but I'm not special, there's a lot of us."

"Doomer. You think I'm somehow involved in a conspiracy against you?"

"Well, you're not just a pretty face."

He blushed and it was adorable. Adorable? I scrubbed my eyes.

"People, or that thing, are after you?"

"Yes. There are those who want to destroy me to save the world, and those who want to destroy me to end the world. I'm fucked. My question is where do you fit in to that?"

He didn't answer. Rubbing my thumbs against my forefingers, I thought, but Church put his hand on my wrist with his eyes on my fingers.

Heat shimmered around us, warming the air, and the light scent of smoke hung over me. The rippling grew hotter before I opened my hand flat.

"Cool trick," he murmured.

"Sorry."

"Don't be." Keeping his eyes on my wrists, he swallowed. "Occasionally I'm asked to look into strange disappearances. Unexplained events."

"Such as?"

Church kept his hand on my wrist, circling his thumb over the inside. "Your mother's death. People who vanish. Most of it is easily worked out, but some things I don't find the answers for. I was asked to look into the break-in at a cottage. The one your mother tried to steal from. When I mentioned the Mirrorwell, I was told to let it drop."

"Huh. Clever. They can use you without attracting attention."

"Who?"

Clearing my throat, I pulled away and started cleaning up.

"Who?" He sounded desperate and yet restrained.

"Hunters. Humans. Men mostly. That's how it started. Men would track and hunt all the different kinds of witches. They know nothing other than what they decide is truth. Often, they're super religious. Nothing more dangerous than a man who thinks he speaks for god."

"They want to kill you."

"And you, apparently."

"I have to give the solicitor an update."

"Say I burnt down Witworth, but you don't know where I am."

I pulled on my coat, shivering, I felt so cold. Standing in front of him, entranced by something sad in his warm eyes, I reached out. His stubble felt nice on my hand as I caressed his face. I loved the texture of men. With a soft kiss to the corner of his mouth, I regretted that this was how we met. So strange.

He would've been fun in other circumstances.

He pulled in a breath and stepped back. "I have this feeling like... I don't know. It's weird."

"Like you're being compelled?"

"Yes."

"Fight it."

"I don't want to." He took my arm and stood close to me. "I have a really bad feeling. I felt it when we met. There's this compulsion to you but I feel like I've done something wrong." He frowned as he searched my face.

"Welcome to my life."

He came closer.

CONSUME MY LITTLE DEATH

slumped, torn between wanting to flee, and the impulse to stay near him. Touch him. The persuasive want that crawled through me wasn't my 'just fuck them and be done' feeling when the fancy took me. No, this was more. My body pulsed in the latent desire he seemed to wake in me.

His eyes were set on my mouth.

"Why are you looking at me like that?"

He stepped nearer with a shy smile and licked his lips. "The longer we spend in each other's company the stronger the feeling gets. You're an astonishing sort of person." His smile widened.

It felt like magic and a lie, but also utterly right.

He ran his finger along my arm and took my hand. Warm and anchored, my heart thudded.

"I don't do this."

"I bet you say that to all the girls."

His face hovered close to mine. "I'm not very good at flirting or... you know. I don't have a girlfriend or-"

"Would you like to be with me?"

The deep flush of his cheeks was too cute. I wanted to take him in my arms and be sweet. I was not sweet in any way shape or form. I leant back a little.

Church took my hand, taking a little breath, focused on where our fingers touched, and led me through to the bedroom. I couldn't take my eyes off him, and tension vibrated between us. The bed took most of the space in his bedroom, and I dumped my things on a chair. Grim flashes of the last few days filtered in and I closed the curtains before turning to him.

Mother's face in the chapel of rest. The altar. I shuddered.

He stood unsure, trapped somehow. I wanted to think of other things and focused on him. I popped my jeans' button and he took a breath, unmoving.

"We don't know each other..." He pulled his eyes up when I eased the jeans down over my hips and stepped out.

I moved closer, and he flushed before licking his lips.

"I'm not okay." He swallowed and expelled a breath. The lost look there of distant horror pulled at me.

Church bent over, taking a few breaths, and shivered.

I smoothed my hand over his back. "It's catching up with you, but this is how it is for me. Though, normally there's a lot more sitting about between events. Come. It'll be okay, I don't have to do anything. I promise. I'd like comfort, if you want."

I climbed in, leaving my top on and patted the mattress as I curled up. A clean, soft bed was heavenly. Closing my eyes, I snuggled in, and a few seconds later I heard movement. I smiled as the bed dipped. I cracked an eyelid. He had a tee and boxers on, and I thought he was the most adorable human. I'd never thought that about anyone, especially a man.

"Are you okay?" I asked.

"I've never seen anything like it. Everything your mother believed is real. You're real. That thing was real."

I shuffled closer, urged him onto his side and spooned him, pressing my thighs to the back of his. Surprisingly firm and rough with hair. He was so still as I draped my arm over his waist that it nearly made me laugh.

"Tell me," I mumbled against his back.

I inhaled his scent deeply, my body relaxing. It wasn't the usual human smell, and not Other, but it was good. Soothing.

With a sigh he started talking, figuring it out in hesitant thoughts, the sound of his voice in his chest rumbling against my face. "I've heard things and met people who felt off, but I've never seen anything like that. I don't understand how these things exist, and people don't know." He tensed, and his heart beat a little harder.

I squeezed him lightly. "It's okay. The knowledge will settle. We choose not to be seen, and the world doesn't want it to be reality, and even when things happen, it's dismissed."

I let him process it, but it'd take time. It mattered that he accepted me, I didn't know why, but it did.

"I'm more than a witch, and that isn't really the right term for what we are. More than human, our spirits are strong, it gives us our power and distinguishes us from mortals. We're hard to kill, live a long time, and even when we die, we tend to hang around."

"But you're not just that either."

"No. I'm infinitely worse." I ran my arm over his chest.

"What's going on here?" He put his trembling hand over mine, holding it there.

"You've gone through a reality-shattering day really, lots to process, and I'm attempting to comfort you."

"Oh." He took a deep breath. "I suppose I have."

"Is it working?"

"Kind of. You're sweet." He nestled closer.

"Ha, no. I'm a monster."

"You're beautiful," he whispered.

I smiled into his back. "Lie."

"Would a monster do what you're doing right now?" He turned his head a little.

"Well, I admit it's selfish."

"Is it?"

"You're not wholly repugnant."

He laughed, soft and deep. "I've been alone for a long time, and in my job I've never fit anywhere. It's hard for me to connect. When I saw you at your mother's house, I thought you seemed so lost. Like me."

"I am. I don't know what's going to happen, but it's not good."

"I have this terrible feeling. I've had it for a long time." He shifted to face me; his silver-grey eyes darker in the dimness. "The end is coming, and the small things don't matter. Then I realised they do because it's all there is. Makes us know we're alive, and I want to connect and then can't. I'm trapped, looking in."

"Church, that's exactly how I feel."

"You can call me Edward."

"Doesn't suit you. Church does. You feel safe and light. A sanctuary." I frowned.

His lips parted. "I shouldn't want to kiss you."

I gave him the smallest smile. "Sometimes after a terrible thing that shakes your understanding of the universe or mortality, one needs a connection. It anchors us again."

"You're also a client."

"You're not paying me."

"I'm supposed to be investigating you."

"Now there's an offer." I smirked.

He laughed, cheeks flushing. "What do you want?"

"You to get some rest. I have a feeling you're going to need it." I leant over and kissed the corner of his mouth.

Church didn't move.

"I'm so drawn to you." My lips brushed the slight stubble of his jaw, but I moved away.

He pulled me back, eyes on my lips, and kissed me. Gentle, sweet almost. He needed something good, and I was probably not the best person to give him that, but I pressed harder, putting my tongue in his mouth.

With his hands around me, body flush against mine, the lust I'd kept repressed lashed out. I rolled him onto his back, pulling my top off. He stilled, gripping my thighs as I took off my bra.

He ran his hands up my waist. "You're gorgeous. And a little frightening." He gave me a needy look as his lips parted.

"Only a little?" I gripped the hem of his tee. "Do you want me?"

With his mouth wide, eyes fixed, he panted. "Yes."

Looking down on him, I pulled his t-shirt off, and put my hand in his boxers, gripping him tightly. He hardened in my grip, and he was perfect. He arched up.

He pulled his underwear down, both of us scrabbling to undress, and I sank onto him, holding his wide-eyed gaze, and I felt powerful.

My mouth watered as I settled, filling my emptiness, my busy mind never satisfied, and for a moment, I had what I needed. Light filled my heart, lightening my spirit. More than just transitory connection, it was wonderful. The moments passed in slow motion, every touch and movement a profound delight, important. In my mind, he glowed, a pure golden cast of sun over us, warm and close.

I rode him unabashed, all the way up and down, slow to start, relishing the feel of him, and then harder, rougher until all he could do was hold on and brace.

I scratched his chest, leaving thick red marks. He lifted his hips, lost to pleasure.

Pleasure came easy for me, always had, and I came hard and deep, soothing the chaos within, never taking my eyes off him. Church kept up in rough breaths and desperate hands. He was delightful as he thrust up following my orgasm, face red, and came.

So beautiful. My heart squeezed.

We collapsed down, and he silently pulled me close, kissing me with so much tenderness as the light dimmed, I wanted to cry.

For a long time after cleaning up, we lay there, touches and kisses exchanged like language, and he said everything beautiful to me. We'd been hasty and foolish, and I didn't care. Church wasn't a mortal, couldn't be. I'd had a lot of sex, and it had never been like that. He fell asleep quickly, and I luxuriated in the sound of his heart and steady breaths. That beat was the most important thing, and I had to protect it at all costs; I knew it in my marrow. Lulled, I closed my eyes.

The day had waned when I woke, and the room vibrated in warning.

Church was sat up, body tensed. "Get dressed."

I grabbed my clothes, as did he.

"What is it?" I yanked on my clothes.

"Attack." He kept his eye on the door.

I heard them, and crept out to the hallway to listen, motioning for him to stay back as we moved through to the front door.

With a bang, everything went to shit.

KNOCK, KNOCK HERE COMES THE APOCALYPSE

vibrated. From within my flesh, wet and squelchy, my newly active companion writhed and cried out. My body contorted, sending Church to the ground with a thump. The room shook.

The altar flickered in my vision before me, and I heard my mother weep. My outstretched and rigid hand touched the goo that wanted me, and everything went still and silent. I let my breath out in a slow whisper, and I was gone; wrenched out of physical existence. I had no form, just thought and vision, but it warped around me like a dream. Frames of action blending from all directions, and I felt nothing; no taste or sound or smell, only images.

The door was kicked in, and I viewed myself from afar, but present as a ghost or spirit. I stood next to Church and leant down. He looked at me and then at other me.

"Time to move." I didn't know if he heard, but he understood.

Three men, all in bland suits with indeterminate white faces and imbued with some preternatural abilities, were on me in a flurry of violence.

A fourth appeared in the smashed in doorway, attacking Church. He punched him square in that perfect jaw. Other me raged, throwing off the attackers and dived over, tackling his assailant to the floor.

Church held his jaw, scrambled up, and hurried back to the bedroom.

"Take my coat and things. We need them." I watched my body take blows.

He grabbed my stuff, then peered through the doorway as my body ripped one of my attackers inside out. Blood and gore spewed out, spattering the walls and soaking the carpet. The humans were woefully unprepared. If they weren't trying to kill me, I'd almost feel sorry for them.

"Window."

Church threw it open. My body smashed into the wall, creating a hole into the bedroom, dust sticking to the blood of the dead man who landed on the floor.

Church stared at the body of me. She was formidable.

Another human tried to stab me, but she moved too quick to see. The human's spine snapped, and he fell. The third ignited in flame, letting out a scream as he flailed.

The piercing smoke alarm went off, and Church shook off his shock, grabbed a bag already packed from the bottom of his wardrobe and threw our things out. He climbed out and dropped down to the ground. At least it was only the first floor.

My body followed him and leant through the window. I recoiled. "I don't think I want my body back." Separated from it, I saw for the first time the true monster I was. I knew what my mother feared, what she locked away, and saw Witworth's desire for my use.

In this spirit form, I was cleansed and made of light. Untainted with evil. It was beautiful, euphoric almost. I revelled in the feeling, time meant nothing, and there was just this.

Church looked up at us from below, and my body crawled out the window and dropped down.

"Adaline." He backed away.

I came back to the moment with Church's lovely but bruised face staring up at me.

Everything went black.

$$\triangle \ \triangle \ \triangle$$

I woke in a car. Sticky and cold. Shuddering, I gagged.

"Hey, it's okay." He drove frantically, spattered with blood.

I looked at my bloodied hands with a blank mind. My head hurt. "Stop," I slurred.

He pulled over, mounting a pavement, and I stumbled out, retching, throwing up bile. Church handed me a bottle of water and a pack of wet wipes. I looked in the little mirror inside the sun visor. My hair and face were plastered with blood and gore.

"I need more than these." But I started wiping my face down.

His jaw ticked as he held the steering wheel. I felt the fear and horror in him. He puffed out a breath and slumped. "Where do we go?"

"I need a minute to think."

"So? What the fuck was that?"

"I have no idea. Never happened before." I side-eyed him.

"But you can guess?"

Guess? Yes. My mother's unwillingness to leave me with Rhere made sense. I barely touched that stuff in the altar and my hitherto quelled demon ousted my witch spirit from my body. "That the dark part of me is gaining in strength. That the prophecy, for once, might be right." I leant back, tasting the coppery tang of blood and bile. Suspicion tumbled through me. I was provoked to defend Church. I can't imagine he'd trust me after seeing that.

"How many prophecies are there?"

I drank the water, but it didn't help with the taste. "Dozens, at least ten in the last few years. I mean, you predict enough, and you're going to be right at least once."

"I suppose."

"Do you have my bags?" I dug out a wet, spongy blob from my ear and used another wet wipe.

"On the backseat."

"We have to get out of here."

He started the car again and pulled off.

The dull day whizzed past us. Quiet and desolate. Birds lined power lines, the town asleep and still. Such a strange thing to see. It felt like it was already over, and I'd missed the war.

"I need food." My vision mottled.

We pulled into a petrol station and he filled the car and went in.

In the quiet, I kept coming back to his scent. It was irritating me that I couldn't place it or rationalise being so drawn to him. Of all the shit that just happened, it was that fact I couldn't stop thinking about.

I narrowed my eyes against the low sun as I got out and stretched and noted how few people were around. They looked panicked and skittish. Loaded cars filled with supplies. The taste of their fear overpowered the lingering one of blood and demon. I spat and rinsed my mouth with the last of the water.

"Where do we go?" He offered me a sandwich as he got back in with a carrier bag of food.

We had no choice, and I told him where to go. It was a risk taking him, but maybe Len knew what Church was. We headed southwest and by the late afternoon, entering a dingy post-industrial landscape of dead factories, and abandoned history, we passed through unscathed. Humanity had long fled this place, leaving it to us. Beyond cracked tarmac and tall grasses snaking up steel fences, the road became other. Lush lanes, laden with autumn fruits, well-rutted, and inhabited by cawing crows, who signalled our arrival.

"Where is this place?" He scrunched his face up, leaning forward as he navigated the lane.

"It's not... reality as you know it. It's a glamour."

"What's that?"

"Magic that draws power from a witch or thing that casts a spell of appearance, space, reality or time," I murmured, narrowing my eyes. Something about mother's cottage. Something I was missing, but my head was too muzzy to think clearly. Len could help me.

We'd barely spoken as I directed him, and the weight and throbbing in my limbs consumed me. I wanted a bath and to sleep for about ten hours. Too heavy and solid, I wanted the free state without my body.

We found the closed way to Len's house and juddered down a winding holloway, branches tapping the car as we went.

I tried to figure how to go about this.

The last time I saw Len, he had another name and body. We'd kept in touch at first, but knew it was dangerous.

There were no cars or signs of modernity as we pulled up to his ivy-covered brick house. Smoke lightly puffed up into a fading sky from a tall chimney. I'd only visited once when he first came here before transitioning.

Len opened the front door, leaning on the frame. I fell out the car, my limbs uneven, and Church helped me up. Not wanting to cling too much, and yet needing to grab hold of him, I dragged my gaze from Church to Len.

Len's contented smile vanished, and he tilted his head. Poker-straight white hair hung down his back. A loose knitted jumper fell off one shoulder, and he wore leggings. He'd always been deathly thin, but he'd filled a little. Still pale though. He looked good.

"Old friend, what's happened?"

I blinked, unable to speak.

He pulled me into his arms, and I held onto him with what strength remained.

Held up by both of them, he and Church got me inside. His house was crammed with shelves and jars, potions and hanging herbs and plants, and felt comfortable as they led me upstairs. They stripped me and got me under the hot water of the shower while I passively let them. Despite the heat, I shivered, watching the blood rinse off me into the water. Nobody spoke.

Len murmured after a few minutes, and I looked into his eyes. Pale silver, sweet and kind but wary. Afraid. Afraid of me.

Once clean and dry, I dressed in faded black jeans and a slouchy long-sleeved tee, and we went down. Something about the air lifted the dark weight from my heart, and I could move better.

A few birds darted and hopped on surfaces as Len made us tea. A young fox nestled in a basket by the window. "He was a pup when his mother died, and he was injured," Len said.

"Have you gone full earth-hippy?" I twirled some hanging bunches of herbs.

He laughed, light sparkling in his eyes. "Remember when we used to sneak out and go clubbing? Old W would get her bitch knickers in such a twist. She used to smack me with that cane. When she caught us kissing?" Len whistled.

"Girls cannot be intimate." I imitated her clipped tone half-heartedly.

"Her face when I told her I wasn't a girl." Len passed out mugs of tea. "I haven't seen or spoken to anyone from that place in more than ten years, so why have you brought this evil to me?"

My skin prickled. "Mother died. I burnt Witworth to the ground."

Len didn't seem surprised, in fact, I guessed he knew I was coming. "I have to ask where you stand and what you know."

"They wanted me to align, so I set it on fire. Killed Matilda. Went to Rhere's, which did not go well. Hunters are gearing up. Mortal disease is coming. It's already begun."

Len sipped his drink, as did a silent and increasingly horrified Church, and I took a deep breath of hot fresh scented tea.

I drank deep and everything didn't seem so bad. "I was told to trust you."

"Oh, sweetie. Maybe you were lied to."

The heady sweetness hid a bitter taste, and my mouth went numb. "Yeah, I have a feeling." I screwed up my face. To my side, Church fell off his chair.

"I'm sorry. I have to be sure."

I'd made a terrible mistake. Again.

I woke up on a comfortable bed and watched a mouse climb across my stomach. I went to pick the little thing up, but my arms were strapped to the posts.

Rested and content, though a little muzzy, I didn't panic or fight. I tested my bindings. They were comfortable at least. The small room was bare other than the bed and a chair next to a chest of drawers, in which sat Deera, who was knitting. Her large thick-framed glasses perched on her nose, and she was rounded and soft, with her dark tawny skin glowing. Motherly, but her age a mystery. At least a hundred, maybe two. I'd only met her a few times, and we'd barely spoken. She was an historian.

"You're awake."

"What the fuck?" I swallowed.

Deera paused. "Len doesn't trust many people. Especially not Doomers."

"Fair." I stretched, trying to shift the mouse off me. "Would you mind?"

Deera looked up, her fingers still click-clacking away. "Ah, poor thing." Setting aside her knitting, she picked up the twitchy rodent and put it down, letting it scamper off. "Bethany is here too. We're having a meeting."

"Yes. I assumed as much. Where's Church?"

"He's comfortable. A human, really?"

"He's not bad as far as they go. Listen, I'm not going anywhere, could you let me out?"

"No. Adaline, look at me." Deera's soft voice made me uneasy. "Lines have always been crossed and tested. We seek our places and find our paths and do what we must to find our boundaries, agreed?"

"Yes."

"The thing is, your boundaries are not the same as anyone else. Your power is like no other. I think you're closer to the Well Guardian than anyone else in terms of power and are yet untested. Your mother hid much from us and she cannot protect you now. What you are is feared. That isn't your fault. What you are will, of course, affect who you become in that. You're so young." She put her hand to my cheek.

"The thing in me is awake."

"Yes. We know. That is why you're not dead. We're convening." She stood up straight.

"We're having a fucking trial? Are you shitting me?" Retaining dignity while strapped to a bed was a challenge.

"I'm sorry. You will be able to speak. No-one wants this to be where we are, but it is. Things are moving. As a people, we need to make decisions. Unify. Act."

I looked away. She was right. In her position, I'd do the same. We cannot always help or change our natures, and I knew what my fate would be.

Deera went back to her knitting while I considered my impending death.

ENTER OH SACRED ONE AND LOVE ME

Deera left me, and despite my worry for Church, restraints and shock, I slept. There comes a point where things just are and happen. My whole life was bathed in horror, and I was tired.

The sun set as I woke from a dream I couldn't hold on to, casting murky orange light across the fields and hills. A clear night rose. My shoulders ached from lying in my position but remained still as I heard people move about downstairs, and when the moon was bright, two witches I didn't know came. I tasted their fear of me, yet I was calm.

"Don't be afraid; I will do no-one here harm."

"We have to bind you," one said, avoiding looking at me.

I laughed. Such trivial magic. "If it makes you feel better, go ahead."

The two strangers glanced at each other, and I kept a straight face. Sort of.

They bound me in a rope, and it was cold on my skin. A skittering of images crossed my vision, and I think they glimpsed something of the monster I am. They stepped back before taking me outside. In the dark, a large bonfire raged, which probably wasn't wise on their end.

I was led to a circle made of white ashes, set out before the fire. I knelt on the cold, damp grass, missing my coat. To the side, I saw Church, who was bound and gagged on his knees. He met my eye and nodded slightly, though he was tense and panting with firelight glowing across his skin.

Before me, Len looked sad, as everyone did. A wealth of regret within each person I knew. Except I didn't know everyone.

A woman, unearthly in her beauty approached. She had pale silver eyes, almost like clear water, and she was so opposed to me, I repelled her like a magnet. She smelt old, different, but looked so young.

Len stepped forward. "This is Annabelle."

I slumped, she was familiar, and I knew who she was, though I didn't understand where the knowledge came from. "The witch of the Mirrorwell."

"Yes, but I am not your enemy," she said only to me before addressing the crowd. "The Court has gathered for the first time in over a hundred years to test Adaline Greyling, child of the Door."

As my sight adjusted to the dark and firelight, I saw a myriad of genders, ages, and power surrounding me. I'd never known the purity of uncorrupted power without malice before and it closed in around me.

I'd never felt part of my kind, of anything. I was banished for the dangerous power I bore, and I swallowed that shame. Not of Court or the Manor, yet I knew both. Witworth Council would have destroyed me, but the Court wasn't intent on it or I'd already be dead. Hope kindled, and my demon listened.

I swayed, my eyes rolling back. My sight flickered as I gazed at the black sky. The stars were gone with the firelight, but I felt Rhere with me. The altar flashed before my eyes. I strobed in and out of my body, fighting for control, the demon nipping at me. I won out, finding my power.

"You destroyed the Manor."

"Yet I didn't. The Door endures, doesn't it?"

Annabelle almost smiled. "I knew Lady Witworth when she was a young apprentice witch. She was an arrogant creature, pious in her dedication to what we are: crusaders of light and defenders of humanity. And she fooled everyone. High Witches, you included, are powerful and pure, but you harbour the enemy in your bones." She entered the circle, and the fine powder rose up and scattered into the wind as she knelt opposite me. "Yet you aren't like her. You chose a different path and resisted your fate."

"You don't know anything about me," I sneered.

"I know so-called Doomers hold powers not normally held by our kind. I know you've worked for Witworth Council. I know your mother shunned them and us even as one of our agents. We need answers."

The fire popped and cracked in the silence.

"When Johanna married the revered Percival and took name of Witworth, we thought the Door would be safe, but Court moves slowly, we became complacent, and our investigation failed. What you did has set into motion a chain of events that you do not understand."

"Can we get on, it's restless."

She glanced behind her where a man stood. Tall with dark hair and eyes. I sniffed the air. "He smells of the dark."

"He had a seed of our enemy born, like you. But he is human. That you exist is everything the evil wants."

"I know. You have no idea what that place was like, what they did to us. The people who died, the babies born as monsters like me if they survived. The things I've done kept me safe, alive, and stopped me going into that thing. Do what you want, I don't care."

My demon caressed me from within, thriving on my anger. *Love me*, it said in a sweet kiss. *Never be alone again, love me.* I let my tension go and swayed in a bold seductive caress. For a second, I knew oneness and peace. I cried out, leaning forward. It'd be so easy to burn my binds, burn them all. Church squirmed, bringing me around. With a growl, I tensed. It relaxed within as I shut it out.

"But you are the only one as yet to tap into their power. It's strongest in you. Possibly strong enough to really be the one."

"Then you cannot permit me to endure, can you?" I kept my tone level.

Annabelle didn't answer. Another stepped beyond the fire, and real power vibrated from her. Her dark brown skin and sleek beauty radiated, and she commanded everything around her. Annabelle glanced back at her before focusing on me.

Squirming against the chafing bindings, I glanced at Church. "Do one thing. Let him go. He's only mortal and done nothing. I swear. I'll do what you want."

"He's proven a little difficult. We don't want to kill you. We want to know what is within you. Know what it knows, test you and its power." Annabelle put her hand on my chest, and I writhed.

"I'm not sure it'll let you." In a moment of clear doubt, I wondered how much of me was poisoned by the evil and how much was just bitter resentment. Where was that line?

Smoke from the fire drifted over us, the heat licking me in the cold. I itched in discomfort.

"I'm a mirror witch, but we of the water know potions. Like your mother."

I cut her a sharp look.

"This is power I crafted with the help of others, and there is only one of its kind. It will make you more... amenable." Annabelle brought out a vial and put it to my lips with our gazes locked. I could have told her there were at least half a dozen of them in my coat but drank it in one gulp, trusting these people, hoping my fate wouldn't be over just yet. I let the liquid coat my mouth and focused on Church as Annabelle stood. His eyes were pained and worried. The crisp, sweet taste eased down my throat, and I relaxed. The fire blurred, and the monster of my flesh was calm.

The witch with Annabelle chanted, her power shuddering in the air. Cold rose from my feet upwards, I raised with it, but my body was weighted; heavier and heavier, sinking into the ground. Annabelle muttered, her chant rising with the other witch.

I turned, my spirit a series of images as it was before, stuttered into being and out again, and then quiet.

No sounds or feeling, no warmth or texture. Only conscious existence.

I floated nowhere and everywhere, and before me, emerged a rippling glass door, yet it wasn't fully realised. Around me and indistinct, open marshland materialised, and before it a figure stood. They were heavily robed and with great power. The words that were spoken rang clear in a language I didn't know. The ground solidified, mist rolled in with a cold wind, and the sweet sickly scent of death hung in the damp air.

How these things came to pass laid bare. People worshipped a god; not from this reality, but another, old and dark and ancient.

"It's not real." A presence became dense beside me, looming and tall.

I turned my head. "Rhere?"

He smiled. "This is my memory, I'm not sure how you're in it." He looked me up and down.

"I'm having a trial."

He raised his brows a little. "Oh. How's that going?"

"I'm probably going to die."

"I think that's unlikely. Did you touch it? The liquid in my altar." We both watched a murky procession of mortals trudging to their sacrifice and death. The chanting figure cut the throat of each mortal, their blood a gift, and bodies lost to the water.

"About that." I couldn't look away from the horror.

"That is what I thought." He slumped. "I am sorry. The demon has gained strength?"

"Yes."

"Then it is lost."

"I wish my mother was here."

"Call her."

As I turned to him, the marsh pulled me down in a crushing hold, pulling to the multitudes of the dead. I reached for Rhere, but he was gone, and the robed figure turned, arms high, eyes vacant. In the distance, yet more hapless souls came, plodding and drawn to the power and their sacrifice. Each human was killed, their blood pulling a tiny spectre of the Door into being, bodies strewn underfoot, bleeding out into the boggy water as they sank.

I struggled, unable to scream, pulled down and falling under into darkness, up became down and I tumbled into nothing. When I stilled, dizzy and confused, I was perched like a spider on the ceiling of a black and white tiled room. Everything stilled around me. I smelt beeswax and dust. Panelled walls, a magnificent clock ticked, and a man drew back a red curtain, spilling open time, and stepped through the Door. It purred in the nothing as it made love to the man, taking him into the darkness. Longing to join them, I watched with brutal loneliness eating at my heart.

He emerged, beautiful and reborn and bathed in the death to come. He turned and looked up at me, eyes black, and he hissed.

The vision vanished, and I was sucked up in a rush of movement and arrived at Witworth but before the Manor was built. A gathering of song and fire deep in ancient woods. The Door, this one flat and circular, was as familiar as home and family. It would seduce me too, whispering in the dark, calling to its children.

I shuddered and turned away.

All portals were different, and behind each one, a singular being. Small Doors, large Doors, powerful demigods, weak and petty demons, all of them clamouring from the other side in bitter anger. I started crying, the despair overwhelming.

I wanted to flee and find refuge in the light.

Church's face came to mind as I trembled, focusing on his ridiculous jawline, the calm I felt with him, the feel of him between my legs, and his sweetness under me.

It grew quiet, and the gathered were looking at me, a sacrifice already made, blood saturating the Door. I covered my mouth as it opened, and I knew the far-reaching reality of their plan.

Recoiling, I screamed as I had never done. The terror and devastation came all at once, in one terrible moment; not abstractly, not with vague statements of the end, but true death. The world quiet and bereft, souls devoured, and nothing but horror scorching the earth.

I thrashed, desperate to get it out. Knowing something because it is part of one's reality doesn't show perspective, not even when I came out of my body did I understand. Not in more than thirty years of existence had I comprehended. Bumbling through, braced, closed off, shut down in anticipation, and there it was. I knew in brutal starkness.

I couldn't stand it. I fell back into myself and reality with a sharp wrench, and into the arms of Annabelle and wept.

"Estelle," I whispered through my tears, sobbing a breath. "Estelle."

"Yes, child?"

For the first time since I was a little girl, I looked at my mother.

MY GOD, MY MOTHER, MY CHILD

n my mother's house, I was quiet and rarely spoke; I was afraid to. Estelle looked for signs in every uttered word. She muttered quietly to herself while I played with little dolls and toy cars.

She made magic in sparkling vials and put them to my lips like medicine. Her potions tasted like Palma Violets. When I made them, they tasted like bad gin. She'd work blessed water into a thick syrup, glittering and bright; their mystery so alluring.

I'd help her as she bent matter to her will, capturing it, keeping it suspended in herbed liquid for all time.

"Look," she'd say, "this one is so dangerous it can kill a witch, and this one can heal. There is so much power contained, and you must never play with them." Her tone was serious, but she kissed my forehead. A fond memory.

But always the pacing in agitation. Sometimes she'd be kind. Weeping quietly, smoothing my hair back. The strongest sense of her was when she'd sing to me in a sweet melodic trembling voice. The memory was acrid and fuelled me.

I knew I was a monster in the literal sense. But she was strong, made of iron and grief. Women like her are forged, and those that follow them must be hard or fail.

I never learnt maths or geography, nothing; my world was the damp house and woods. She taught me about power. Magic. I learnt so much in those years, but mostly I learnt how to lie and keep secrets.

It would have been easy to vilify or sanctify her though I could do neither. She had an impossible role, and my sympathy for her matched my resentment.

I harboured such anger, and for a long time I let people think it was for her. But it never really was; it was at her being taken from me, at the power I suppressed, at the Witworth Council. At myself. None of that mattered now. Estelle, her name now free in my heart, was with me.

"There, there my girl, it's all right now." She came close, surrounding me in wispy greyness.

"You should have drowned me." I remembered her at bath time and saw the impulse to end it as she rinsed shampoo from my hair with a plastic jug.

"I loved you."

She felt real as the sun on a spring day. Light through cloud.

"I tried to help you." Her voice caught.

"Witworth was so dangerous." I leant up, and she looked young. Her hair wild and long as I remembered it and threaded with flowers, she was luminous like Percival was.

Annabelle left us, and Estelle soothed my back. I almost felt it.

"The world comes to a crossroads, paths diverge, and nothing is certain. You're not the one. But you're the strongest. I always knew it. To protect you..." The pain in her eyes dimmed her light.

"I don't want this."

"None do. You have been divided from yourself to survive. But you are both things, witch and demon. These are not bad. You choose the path, but I had to bring them together." Such a tender voice and soothing tone.

To the side, Percival appeared, and I smiled, licking the tears from my lips. "You're here." I didn't know if anyone saw either of them.

"A spirit is drawn to power, and I am drawn to you." He bowed his head.

Estelle stood with him, and I turned back to Annabelle. With her head lowered, she deferred to the other witch before speaking to the crowd. "The High Witch. Our Queen. Elected above of all, speaks."

I expected her to be taller, but she was rumoured to be four hundred years old.

"Stand." She wore a silver dress flowing like moonlight and in one hand was my dagger, and in the other, she held a sword. Long and broad, down its centre was a stream of the same realm glass my blade was made of.

I stood, swaying. I felt the smoke permeate me, a cold breeze drifting over us, the fire crackling over the silent gathering.

"How did you come into possession of this?" She raised my dagger.

Clearing my throat, I glanced at Church. "I went to Rhere, the Well Guardian. We spoke, and I looked into the well. I saw its true nature, and it touched me."

Murmurs. The Queen looked sad. "Yet you lived?"

"It didn't consume it, but it was enough to waken the demon. I've always suppressed it. Mother knew it would keep me alive until I was able to master it."

"Have you?"

"No, it was a few days ago."

"What did Rhere say?"

"Lots of things but he confirmed the end was here, and that I had a part in it."

"Your powers?"

I turned to Estelle, who watched passively. "Fire. Potions, a bit. I see the dead. Oh, and apparently, I can detach my witch spirit from my body for the demon to take over and I become a killing machine." I shrugged.

No-one spoke. The Queen stared, and I smiled awkwardly.

"Hunters have increased their attacks."

"Yes. They used to be merely mortals but not now. They're taking power, I suspect from corrupted witches. I can taste it. I was attacked in broad daylight."

"Did you kill it?" She held up the blade.

"Yes. In my defence, they were going to kill me."

She tilted her head. Her full natural hair haloed her. "They? How many human hunters have tried to kill you?"

I had to think. "Um... ten, no, fourteen if you count the ones today."

"Is it possible your friend works for them?" She looked at Church as he struggled.

"If he does, it's not knowingly."

His chest rose and fell harshly, and I smelt his terror.

"He's not one of them. He could have taken my dagger and killed me a number of times but didn't."

"What if I killed him?"

I looked at her. "I'd end everyone here."

"I see." At a slight turn of the Queen's head, Church was untied but surrounded, he slumped down, eyes set on me.

I smiled at him. Annabelle took the weapons.

"I've had many names over the years. I change them for taste, but I am Musa." Musa stepped closer to me, and though she seemed young, she wasn't. Her flawless brown skin and height belied her age. In her deep black eyes was a wealth of power and knowledge.

She lightly pinched my chin, looking deep into me. The moment drew out and letting my chin go, Musa lowered her eyes from mine. She was afraid.

"Let's go to the next stage." She drew a small circle around us scattering more ash from a pouch held out to her and undid my binds. Raising her arms high, she murmured, swaying, light shining through her.

She came close to me, chin high. "You must prove your allegiance. What do you know? What did you see in the vision I gave you?"

"It wasn't a vision, it was Rhere's memory at first. He showed me the network of portals, and those in them who are waiting. I saw the first door being pulled into reality. Then I was at that door as it is now, and a demon came from the other side into a man."

"Where?"

"I don't know. I also saw Witworth."

She closed her eyes. "There are many doors and purposes. What is Witworth's?"

"Death. Nothing but death."

Musa lowered her head. "There was a Door once, only small in a hot place for which no name remains, and it incited a fanaticism that paralleled any religion. Turned its followers into mindless acolytes. Nothing unusual, but the chaos it inspired spread like poison. The door was destroyed. Only a few have ever been removed from reality, and the cost was immense." Musa closed her eyes. "Some doors are hidden. Others blatant. I do not know this unknown door but now I need to see Witworth."

I shook my head, and she put her hand around my waist. This wasn't going to be good.

SHUDDER BACK INTO THE DARK

Musa sighed her warm breath on my cheek. "Open your eyes."

I didn't want to. Blood and decay and ash. The air vibrated and warmed before cooling again. The acrid burnt smell was gone, and I did what she asked.

The bowels of Witworth were familiar but different. "How are we here?"

"Bending reality and time is the highest ability. Why else do you think I'm Queen?" Her voice was weak.

"Wait, why can't we stop it now or then? Why not do this before and just go back and–"

"It's like a repeat, sort of. It's complicated. Visions do not say all."

"Then why do you not already know everything."

"Because, Door Child, one needs a powerful being or object as a source that's connected to the place. Nothing can be altered. This place was concealed with a glamour, and with its passing, I can now enter." Her voice grew so quiet in the dark; I could barely hear her.

The implications of it turned over as Musa sagged, and her light faded. I put my arm around her and held her up, but my eyes were locked onto the large flat circle that hovered a foot off the floor. Black, not from colour but from an absence. I'd seen people lose all reason when they looked at it for any length of time.

Its reality always made me want to cry; the despair infecting any life near it.

Musa was already weeping. I wanted to say she'd get used to it, but it'd be a lie.

Shuffling brought her around, and we slid into a corner behind us.

"This place is..." Musa covered her mouth.

"Fucking horrendous."

There were no wires or pipes or anything familiar around us, and even the bricks weren't blackened and stained. The stench was the same, sickly rot rising from the wet floor. Our whispers fell to nothing as a door opened and lamplight preceded Lady Witworth, a young one at that. Her dress was straight out of the Stuart era.

Following her was a young woman in a nightgown tethered to a man. They looked dazed and pale. Lady Witworth ushered the couple up a little wooden stair and pushed the prisoners into the Door. They hovered, and the walls seemed to breathe, but the glass shimmered, and atmosphere changed. Heavy and cloying, the limp bodies were pulled in and vanished. Hiding on the stairs was a living, breathing Percival, and I covered my mouth. Always so casually dressed. His long curling hair the same, in fact, he looked the same as his ghost. His eyes were aghast, mouth turned down. His eyes flickered in grief and betrayal.

Startled, he noticed us and raised a brow. Musa squeezed my arm.

Lady Witworth turned holding her lamp up. "Percy?" She called back.

"Is all well, my dear? I thought I'd fetch some wine while you were taking your vigil."

"That would be perfect." She turned back to the portal, now still once again. "All seems well here." She went off.

We didn't speak for a minute, but he approached, and we edged out of our corner. "Well. This is unexpected." He tried nonchalance, but his voice trembled a little, and he led us away down a narrow passage.

In the wine cellar, he grabbed a bottle and leant on the wall. "Well. My Queen."

I managed to stop gawping. "You know her?"

Percival tilted his head with keen eyes examining me. "Our newly appointed monarch entrusted me to monitor the Door and the thing I was obliged to marry." He inspected my clothes with interest.

Musa stepped to him and cupped his face. "How can you see us?"

Percy glanced from her to me and back again.

"You were once my loyal advisor and a great soldier. You had such power."

He tilted his head, eyes widening. "I thought we were more than... Had? When are you?"

"Far in front."

"Then it did not go well."

"I'm loath to say."

"But you've come all this way, be a shame not to." He smiled with such tenderness at Musa.

"That Door took you, or so we were told."

Percival went grey, put the bottle of wine back and selected another. He pulled the cork out and drank. "Might as well drink the good wine then." His face contorted momentarily before drinking again. He set the bottle down, and I thought he might weep. "Be good to get this over with, for I cannot endure more. She tells me nothing, and I receive no word or acknowledgement of my letters."

"I received nothing after the first few, we sent emissaries, but they heard or saw nothing."

Percival drank more wine, torn between despair and fury.

We heard steps, and Lady Witworth stood in the passageway. Musa pushed me back against the wall, keeping me hidden.

"The Witch Queen. With my husband. How interesting." Lady W's mouth pursed in an unpleasant manner, just as it did when I knew her.

"You know I was in the Queen's service." Percy stood.

"I'm sure you still are."

Musa advanced. "And what do you do by serving the aberration you were sworn to destroy? Your appointment was to guard the world against its evil. Now you serve it."

Lady Witworth straightened her back. "You know nothing of the power within it."

"Please, tell me." Musa was all soft honey.

Johanna's eyes flickered. "It wants freedom from the nightmare where it dwells. It means no harm."

"Other than death." Musa shook her head, but before she said more, Percival put his arms around his wife's neck, crushing her as she flailed, and snapped it. In a quick pivot, he smashed the open bottle over her head.

She hissed, black foam bubbling from her mouth, covered in blood and wine with her head at an angle off to the side. She pulled out a knife from her dress pocket, launched at him and stabbed Percival in the neck. He put his hands to the wound, stemming the blood, but it pumped out between his fingers.

Witworth cracked her neck back into place. "Is that the best you can do?" She didn't give Percival a second glance as he crumpled to the floor with a gurgle.

He stood next to me against the wall, shocked as his spirit form flickered into being. "That did not go as expected."

Musa put her hand on Johanna's face, and her eyes rolled back. She flailed before Musa pushed her across the room so hard, she smashed into the brick, debris falling on her and wailing in pain. With a gasp, Musa reached back to me, and we vanished.

Embers sparked, and I threw up sour bile, falling out of the circle. Church hustled away from the others and held me. Musa staggered, shivering.

Everyone was silent. I looked at Percival standing with my mother, and I closed my eyes. "She killed you." I spat acid.

"Ah, I wondered if that's where you went." He shrugged.

"Who are you talking to?" Church produced a tissue from his pocket.

I spat again and wiped my mouth. "Percival Witworth. He's dead. It's a thing."

"He's here?" Musa had her hands on her knees with Annabelle at her side.

He stepped closer, materialising in a more solid form and shimmered so all saw him. People murmured.

"You never told us." Musa had tears in her eyes.

"It is a circle. And it has come around. I guarded the little ones when they came. The council has always been careful since my death. They made the right noises, placated the Court with shrugs and lies, used deceit at every turn. They did enough glamour to stay out of focus. I couldn't leave Witworth before, but all that's left is the door. The power here drew me back from darkness."

"Percy, I'm sorry. I don't understand how you could see us. It's my fault." Musa drew in a sharp breath, tears streaming.

"My dearest Queen, the power of that place affects all. I cannot pass beyond. Everything is stronger and more dangerous." He hovered close her. "It is well and was meant."

She regained her composure. "One of ours was there for a while or watching, but we lost him when the place burnt."

"Who?" I asked.

"Dane. Greying with a beard."

"I saw him at a service station just after I burnt it. Told me to come here, and to go to Church. Told me to trust Len." The floor kept spinning.

"What happened?"

"Something followed me. I think from Witworth or hunters. I should have fought it. I shouldn't have run." My hands shook, and I needed to eat and lie down, my adrenaline ebbing.

"Tomorrow we'll reconvene, it's time to rest." Musa kept her eyes on Percival as he bowed and shimmered away.

Someone grabbed Church, and I growled. "He stays with me."

Musa nodded, and I took his hand, pulling him away. He steadied me as we went up. Our things were on the small bed I'd been tied to. We looked at each other, silent and spent.

Church folded his arms, leaning on a wall, a purple bruise on his cheek, staring at nothing.

"Are you okay, did they hurt you?"

He didn't answer. His eyes were vacant. After a little while, he took a shaky breath. "Sometimes there's so much, you can't take it in. I wonder if the scariest thing is the ghosts or witches, but I think it's the fact the world is probably going to end."

"Right?" I huffed a strange laugh.

His chin trembled, and I wanted to hold him.

Someone brought us food, and we ate a little later. I undressed and climbed into bed, and the tall, lanky man attempted to fit in around me.

"How are you doing?" I asked, lacing my fingers through his.

"I don't know. I'm glad you're okay. All I'm sure of is that I have to be with you. It's the strangest thing."

We'd known each other a few days. Yet he was bound to me, and our fates entangled. My bones vibrated with peace and rightness with his presence.

I knew that wasn't necessarily a good thing.

GIVE OF ME AND THE STARS I BEG

hurch slept. He tossed and turned a little, I'd soothe him, and he'd settle again.

I managed a few hours before shoving my hair up on my head and resisted the need to put my coat back on. I curled up in the chair, eyeing the old doctors' bag.

Out of place, it smelt damp, the leather dried and cracked. The frame of it had been crushed at some point, and it leant to one side.

I'd fought who I was for so long, and I couldn't remain in denial. Musa's use of her dangerous gift with me to see the past stuck. Why go back? Seeing Percival must have been an incentive.

Wrapping my head around that, I found my cigarettes and put an unlit one in my mouth, letting it hang there, and rubbed my fingers along the wood of the armrest, feeling it heat.

I saw Estelle pace on the porch as the room faded from me. I ran along the fence that separated the field from common ground, tapping the posts as I went. All the while she paced and watched.

A blackbird perched on a gatepost at the far end, and I skipped to it. It flapped and squawked in a panic, even though I was nowhere near it, and it flew away.

"Adaline!" Mother's cry echoed over to me. She stood still; hands clasped. Stillness was worse than pacing.

I didn't know why I was so upset, and I sobbed as I ran back to her. She wanted to comfort me, but instead she backed away and ushered me inside.

I nearly lit the cigarette but took it from my lips for a moment.

Those birds feared me. Everything does. Except for Church.

I watched him. A sliver of moonlight fell over his form. Chest rising under the blankets.

A fear, sneaking and incessant, tapped at the back of my mind. A trap, a lie; anything other than what he appeared to be. How could such a perfectly lovely human desire and care for me? He accepted everything so easily. So calm. But he'd seen my worst and then we fucked. That had to count for something. Or nothing.

I rubbed my face and shook it off. I needed to decide what to do next, but planning my next move was useless; I could no more control what was to come than I could the weather. From the bed, Church mumbled and turned over. I turned my attention back to the bag.

Mother left it for me to find, knowing I'd go to the house. I crouched down to it, sliding it out of the dark, almost afraid something would reach out through it. So many old ghosts.

I opened it and stared into the depth of its musty interior as if it could give me the answers I was seeking. Inside was a small ancient book. *The History of Portals.* I'd not seen it in the Witworth library. Setting it aside, I pulled out a handful of vials. The precious light still bright in them.

I wanted to call to her, ask her questions, but not yet, I couldn't face it. She knew that, and she'd wait for me.

With the bag set inside my crossed-legged sit, I shivered, and grabbed my coat, staring at nothing.

"What is it about that thing?" Church was sat up, looking at me.

Taking the cigarette from my lips, I set it carefully on the side. "I lied to you. I'm good at it, and it's my default. I've lied to everyone about everything to stay safe."

Church relaxed against the headboard. "So tell me the truth about something."

The silence never usually bothered me, but I hated that it was hard to fill with the truth. I made my voice work. "The coat was my mother's. I wasn't taken to Witworth but sent, and she readied me to go. She said they'd come, maybe kill her, and I had to go and fight my fate. Never trust. Never love. Never give of yourself. My rules were her rules. We made a big show of it when they came. I cried, she fought.

"In my room was a case, and she packed this coat in it. I was supposed to take the doctors' bag, but they hurried me out and away. She did her best. She hated me, how could she not? Yet, she loved me. Gave me the tools I needed to survive."

We were quiet for a long time. Slipping off the coat, I climbed back into bed and held him. "I'm sorry you've been dragged into this."

"Another lie?"

"A little. I'm glad you're with me, but I'm afraid for you." I caressed his cheek.

Church kissed me, feeling me all over.

I pulled away. "Rest. We'll need it."

We settled down, and I ran my fingers along his scalp with his head on my chest. He murmured before drifting back to sleep.

Laughter woke me, I slipped out of bed and cracked the door open. Pulling on some jeans, I went down. In the kitchen, around the table, were Len, Deera, her wife Bethany, Annabelle and Henry.

"What's this?"

Everyone stilled.

Len got up, fetching another glass and poured me a drink from the jug of the cocktail. "Don't worry, you're safe." He handed me the glass.

I took it.

"I'm sorry. We had to know. I couldn't take the risk."

"I understand. I'd have done worse if I were you, to be honest."

He kissed my forehead, and we hugged.

I sat at the table, shooing a mouse off it. I think this was the only place animals didn't run away in panic from me.

Annabelle smiled and nodded, and I raised my glass.

"Now what?" I drank the sweet yet acidic liquid and grabbed some nibbles from the table.

"Well, the Queen will want to reconvene tomorrow night," Annabelle said, topping up the glasses. "Then decide what our plan will be."

I eyed Annabelle. "So you spent like three hundred years in a demon prison, and you get snapped up as the Queen's right hand?"

"She came personally. There aren't many of our age left. She was established and political when I was learning. In those days we were centralised and had a portal master. We travelled, but the war was slow and cruel, and then there were the human witch hunts. The witches I trained under were murdered. As I understand it, our network fell apart, and we were scattered. Demons escaped through lesser Doors and ran wild. Our kind has been playing catch up ever since."

We were quiet for a while, and I thought. "I guess Witworth plays into that?"

Len cleared his throat. "They orchestrated most of it. Say we're checking this person and then the person disappears or dies. And Witworth says, oh the demons or hunters got them. They gather waifs and strays and corrupt them." He looked at me.

The implications and unease of my part in that were huge. "That is my crime, I suppose. Active role in that, or complicit in its action." I knocked back my drink. "What's Court like?"

"Dull. Lots of talking and more talking. Analysis and data. The internet is fascinating and such a strange thing, but useful for us. Things are different."

"That's very important, but," Len rested his elbows on the table, "tell us about the human."

"I'm not completely convinced he is."

"Why?" Bethany, quiet, pale and blonde with delicate features asked. Her shrewd face was appealing.

"I'm not compelled to them. The opposite in fact. No offence."

"None taken," said Henry.

"What do you think he is?" Deera served some cake, and we dived in.

I was ravenous and ate two slices before drawing breath. I paused with a mouthful. "I don't know. Not a witch, not a demon, but he's something else."

"Or he's just a good person. How many of them have you been around?"

"I mean," I licked icing off my fingers, "you might be onto something."

At a sound on the stairs, I turned.

Church, rubbing his face, joined us. "Am I interrupting?"

"No," Len said, "join us, but there's no seats."

"You can sit on my lap." I patted my thigh.

He laughed, and my heart warmed. He urged me up, and I sat on him.

"In all my life I've never sat on anyone's lap."

"Well, there's a first for you then." With a squeeze to my waist, he took the drink offered to him.

"No hard feelings about tying you up, I hope?" Len asked.

"Um, I'll let you know."

We listened to the table disseminate the events so far, asking me questions, and I told them everything I could. It was good not holding back, and I didn't brace for attack.

"All right," Len slapped the table. "Enough." He got up, put music on and danced a little as he tidied. Deera helped, Henry and Church exchanged cautious glances, and Annabelle stared at me.

I sat back against Church, his chest rising and falling. That small moment pivoted me in a shift of thinking. I'd survived by any means, but things had altered. I wished Rhere was there with wise words and vodka. I saw goodness and hope, and my existence meant loss. All gone and given over to things which had no business in my world. In the past, everything had been against me, but now I was against something. Against the end. Against Witworth.

A plan formed as I sipped my drink. "I have an idea."

People turned to me. Best laid and all that.

BE MY VENGEANCE AND MY WARRIOR

The night went on forever. My breath misted, and I huddled into my coat. The lining was smooth and warm, and the thick exquisite wool as fresh as the day it was crafted with all its magic. The faded but present scent of my mother's perfume and my tobacco clung to it. The long wool collar hugged my neck and brushed my jaw. Its comfort eased my agitation. I needed peace and quiet away from the unnatural frivolity. Behind me, everyone still sang and danced and drank. They celebrated nothing but that they existed for another day. Such joy was uneasy for me. I loved moments on the outside, forever looking in at the party. I'd never be different. Cold wind and rustling leaves were my company in the garden.

With the fire reduced to smouldering ash, the stars were bright. I looked up at them, quiet and still. They roared beyond time and spoke just like Rhere.

Church appeared next to me, he swayed a little and took my hand. I squeezed, beating back the fear and worry, and for a tiny, pristine moment, I had hope.

"Adaline."

"Hmm?" I turned, finding his blank face fixed on me.

"Something bad is going to happen."

I opened my mouth to speak, but from the other side of the ash, a figure appeared. I screamed, not in fear, but a warning, screeching so loud, Church covered his ears, and it carried to the house and beyond.

The figure approached, I felt power come from it, and from around us, more emerged from the dark. I crouched a little, reaching to Church.

They were a collection of scents; witches, demons, no humans, and the familiar stench of Witworth. I scrunched Church's shirt in my fist as others came out of the house with the Queen leading.

One struck at me, but I deflected to the side, eyes fixed on the knife in his hand. If I was alone, these things would already be dead, but Church was mortal, and terror halted me. I hesitated, and then it happened too quick for me to react. My demon was still quelled from the potion, leaving it muted and small.

My friends rushed across the gardens, and two assailants closed in.

I recognised Grant as he lunged forward, thrusting a sword to the hilt into Church's gut. The rush of action skidded to a halt, and time stopped. My heart beat once. It all happened so fast, and my mind turned as quickly. Church would die.

I was death and fury. I attacked.

Church fell to his knees, and I lunged at the monster who took him from me. I threw him high into the air and casting my hand up, set him on fire. Wreathed in flame, he lit up like a firework, flames dripping from him. All stood still in shock. My power revealed. The second assailant gawped up at the molten body, and I ripped the sword from his hand and cut his throat, hot blood spraying me. It cooled quickly as bone disintegrated into ash and floated on the breeze. The garden darkened.

Heat filled the air, shimmering, raging and boiling in my blood until sparks flickered. The dead fire on the lawn re-ignited as I pressed out the pressure in my body in a wave. It threw three attackers into the flames, and I whipped around to face the last two.

Esher and a boy.

I spat the blood that found its way into my mouth and growled. "Where's Witworth?" It wasn't my voice that came out of me; it was something else, dark and oddly itchy.

The Queen appeared at my side, and she feared me. Esher glanced at her but was fixed on me. I took a step and held my hand out to Musa, who passed me her sword. I swung and cut off Esher's head. With her was Abdul. He was a quiet, sweet man, but young. He fell to his knees, awaiting death.

I'd brought him to Witworth myself years ago. Afraid and alone aged eight, I gathered him into my arms after the death of his family, but he was just more fodder for the Door. My fury waned.

In a crouch, I lifted his chin. Pure terror at what had come to him radiated out, making my mouth water. He stared absently at the monster that defeated his purpose.

But I hadn't won. My grief inched in. "Where is Lady Witworth?"

"Not here. Hiding." A tear spilt down his cheek.

"The people who kept you are dead. Join us and be free." I stood, turning away.

The others watched me, and I held out the sword to Musa with a bowed head. Deera and Bethany hovered over Church.

Sluggish and heavy, I walked to him with my spirit out of step. I'd nearly separated as I had before but remained one, yet not entirely anchored. I reached out to him, and my echo caught up. People moved away in silence.

I knelt, and pulled him up, body slippy with blood and face ashen in the moonlight.

I keened with dangerous, vibrating menace. My spirit was quietly waiting as the animal raged in me. Biting and clawing. My two selves wrought on the edge of grief.

My cry grew louder into a roar, my body shaking with power.

Deera, sweet motherly Deera, came close, touching my arm. I bared my teeth, and Bethany stepped forward.

"Let us help him."

I picked him up, his weight nothing and my consciousness vapour-trailed behind as we went back inside. The table was swept clear, and I set him down.

My spirit cleared my body finally. A relief free of the physical pain. I gazed down at Church, so pale and bloodied. Then I saw me. I was the colour of bone, my hair shining, eyes wholly black. I looked like marble, dense and unreal.

My body looked at me, mouth open wide. Like before, in Church's flat, I was light and free. Now with Church dead, I didn't want back in. It seemed so pointless.

"Well. I'm dead then." Church flickered into being. His stuttering visage wavered. "Feels a bit weird."

I touched his cheek, our essences merging in almost electric pleasure. Without connection to the physical world, it was the only sensation. I smiled, holding him in blissed touch.

Everything was quiet, and everyone stared at us.

Their forms were so dense and slow to move.

"Adaline?" The Queen approached my spirit. "You have to come back. You cannot leave your body loose."

My body's hands were clawed, and it twitched.

That thing was the best chance at halting what was coming.

Church smiled at me. "I'm not going anywhere."

I caressed his face and kissed his lips and then willed my return. My body protested, and I don't think it wanted me back either.

Entering my body was a painful squeeze, like diving into water, I fell to the ground and passed out before I could ask what the sudden commotion was.

The weight of physical reality was leaden and painful and kept me still, but I managed to open my eyes.

The smell of magic, smoky and sweet, undercut with muskiness, permeated the air. Church was thrashing, and people were holding him down. A discarded potion vial fell and rolled along the floor.

He'd gone from where he was standing, and I wept.

"Child, move." My mother materialised, and I crawled over to the range, shivering and miserable.

She hovered close, and it was comforting.

"Who is he?" I whispered.

"You care about him?"

"Yes. I shouldn't. He's working for your solicitor investigating me for the insurance policy you set up. Why would you do that?"

Church arched up, body rigid, and the others tried to hold him down.

"There's no policy, and I don't have a solicitor. There's a plan. You must find her."

I glanced at her, confused.

We watched Church sit up, turn, letting his legs swing off the table, and looked right at me.

Len frowned and tilted his head, and everyone stepped away from him. Church clung on staring at me with his head bowed.

I swallowed thickly. "Mortal spirits do not remain, and they cannot see the future."

Who the fuck was he?

AT THE DARK DAWN, A SACRIFICE

Locking my hands around my knees, I watched people keep busy. Tidy up. Patch up Church. Activity buzzed, but I wanted no part of it or anything else.

"Len. I'd like some of that tea to knock me out, please." I said it quietly, but he heard me, and though no-one spoke, there were shared looks and tension, but it passed me by.

Church stared at me, but I kept my eyes on his shoes, all muddied and ruined. Len patted my head as he handed me a mug, and I sipped it, unable to stop shivering.

Mother and Percival hovered unseen, flickering in weakness and trying to comfort me, but I felt nothing other than weight. Bodies are so dense.

Church eased up, holding his middle, shirt open, blood everywhere. He stood over me and held his other hand out.

I raised my face. "Who are you?"

"I don't know." Uncertainty lay in his sad eyes, mouth turned down, and he let his hand drop.

Deera came in from outside, covered in ash. "It could be this place. There's convergence here, and your mother and Percival were able to appear, and usually, the dead only stay where they died."

I didn't believe her.

My eyes flickered, and I stood. "No. You are something other."

"As far as I know, I'm human. Parents, school, work. Just normal."

Deera washed her hands at the sink. "I don't know when there were so many preternatural creatures and power in one place. The Court, all of us, you. The portents told us-"

"Deera." Bethany put her hand on Deera's arm.

"Too late, spill. I've heard this shit before. 'Portents say you are the promised one.'" I mocked the tone always used with me, and I shook. "This deceit has been with me all my life. Everyone has conspired to keep me a secret and keep knowledge from me, but look at this." I roared, throwing my arms out. A beat of silence passed, and I shuddered out a calming breath. "For once, at the end, if it's so important, tell me the fucking truth."

Deera turned to Bethany. "She has to know, after what just happened."

"Tell her." The Queen leant against a far wall, looking spent. I imagine she'd been shoring up the defences with her power.

"A little over two weeks ago, there was a shift. As if something woke. All seers felt it. A veil lifted," Deera said quietly.

I looked at what image remained of mother, and she bowed her head.

Deera went on. "Across the globe, Doors shook, and covens felt the coming storm. In those portents, the portals opened. All of them. They swallowed the world, and you were front and centre bathed in fire and death."

I sat on the floor. Even I saw it. I dreamt of my mother wandering the hills near her house, and she was speaking though I couldn't hear her words. Darkness fell over us, and the land was red, the imploring horror in her eyes chilled me, and I tried to reach her but couldn't. She screamed, or I did. When I woke, I knew she was gone.

I scrambled to the sink and threw up.

Musa stepped forward. "The thing about portents is they're not always what they seem, but so many of us saw you, but not the witch."

I rinsed my mouth, taking a second. "You saw my demon."

"The demon."

"Then my mother tried to steal the Mirrorwell to trap me? I guess. But failed."

As a pale shadow, she spoke to me. "All my life I hid you and your power. I hid you within the house with magic and spells and potions, and my coat. I knew the inevitable would come, I always knew. I tried so hard for you. Gave up everything to fight it because you were a baby, a child, my child. I hoped if I gave you enough tools you could fight, but when the portents came, I knew I was out of time and my plan not ready. I cannot hold on much longer, you must find her." She flickered from my sight, the still images that echoed were of anguish.

The room was silent as we watched her pain and struggle, Percival hovering near her, and her light returned, so brilliant, I winced.

Her voice was deep and echoing when she went on. "The fight came too early. I needed more time to be ready for what is coming. I saw the portents before, for I am a seer. In panic, I exposed myself and you, but not all, there are weapons still. Adaline, my mistake cost me my life, and I failed. My mission was preparing you. Once, there was a portal master, and we needed another." Mother faded, head bowed, as her strength diminished into nothing.

I put my clenched hands to my forehead and pushed back the emotion in my chest. The tea started to kick in, and I gulped the rest of it before getting up. "I can't." I turned back to Church. "You coming?"

He followed.

We stripped in silence, our smoke scented clothes left in a heap on the floor, and in the bathroom, I hung a towel over the mirror; I didn't want my friend to come out and play. We washed up and fell into bed and went to sleep; the apocalypse and questions could wait.

Birds chattered as I opened my eyes and sat up. I needed to know what was in that tea because I felt refreshed. The misty russets of unspoilt autumn filled the view. Church was still out cold.

His chest was purple, but he was whole, whatever that was. After dressing, I sat in the chair, the cigarette I picked out last night still on the side. Felt like a lifetime ago. Next to it was the book from the doctors' bag.

Picking it up, I went down and made some coffee. The place was quiet, and I spotted everyone outside, surveying the damage in the daylight.

I sat at the table, sipping my drink, and opened the book and read a chapter on types of realm travel.

Deera came in, and I shivered. "Ooh, would you like a jumper? I've got a few lying around." From a basket, she pulled one out and handed it to me. A loose-knit in dark purple and I snuggled into its softness.

She joined me, cleaning up the veg she'd picked. "How are you? And how's the lovely Mr Church?" She peered over her glasses.

"Alive, whatever that is. Bruised and out cold." I scowled, tapping my mug. "I need answers. I need to know what to do next. Do we carry out the plan?"

Deera laid out an old handwoven cloth, smoothing it. "I've been thinking about some of the histories."

I glanced up from a page on types of portals. "Yes?"

"Do you know where High Witches come from?"

"No, just that we're a line of ordained power."

"Yes." She rescued a caterpillar from a cabbage and put it out through the window. "In the beginning-"

"Oh good grief." I dropped the book.

Waving a wonky carrot at me, she narrowed her eyes. "In the beginning, there was a war. No people or creatures, but a war of matter, power and force and the unknown. From whence came the demons. They formed two sides, one defeated as they took form, but not wholly cast down, and with their remaining power opened the first portal and came here."

"What's that from?"

"Holdel Foweller's History of Witchcraft, 1633. Documents the history of the eternal war while the middle war was ongoing, and I have two copies. The one we all know, and an original edition."

"I've read that book and never heard that before." I sipped my drink. "Wasn't he a bit odd?"

"Very." She emphasised the word and put the box of clean veg aside and cleaned the table. "He was one of the oldest living. He didn't remember when he was born. Spoke so many languages. He hid our kind from hunters during the trials. Annabelle might have known him. According to Foweller, High Witches are that which came here first. The text was since edited." She pulled a face and went still, staring in thought.

"Why was our history edited?"

Deera leant in. "We've been corrupted slowly and quietly. What do victors do when in power? Control information." She raised her brows over her glasses. "What do you have there?"

Strangely it was a Foweller book too. "Mother had an old doctors' bag. She kept her potions in it. Her bag of tricks. I opened it for the first time and found this." I slid it to her.

"I've never seen it." She turned a page. "These are Foweller's casting patterns for doors and mirrors. This is everything we no longer know about them. He lost all reason after a battle with a demon when he closed an unlocked gateway. It took a great toll on him, and he was chained and made to write everything down in 1698 but escaped and burnt all his centuries of work before ending his life. It's why we only have three remaining texts. And now this one."

"Why would mother have it?"

She didn't answer but leafed through the book and went still.

"Deera, did you know mother?"

She looked up slowly, glancing out the window. "High Witches are slippery. We're scattered and hidden in this modern age, but you know that because you were sent to find us by Witworth. It wasn't always so."

I nodded, clinging to the warm mug.

"I was friends with your mother, once. As Court historian, I travel and gather knowledge. I helped her often, and her fear of Witworth and for you guided everything she did."

I didn't breathe. "I remember you when I was a child."

Tears rimmed her eyes. "I visited the Manor, looking for Estelle and by then I suspected what was going on. What you were. We managed to get some young witches away and hid them. I was so afraid for Estelle, but she was extraordinary. Her gifts were many and powerful, but she wasn't perfect. She had many regrets."

People talked loudly outside, and Len laughed.

"When I was small, I was always so afraid. All I wanted was her to be my mum. When I went to the cottage when I was told of her death, I remembered her without love but with fear and resentment. I couldn't let myself feel anything else for her." I took a breath and my heart hurt.

"And now you feel everything."

Emotion, the pull in my throat and chest for what might have been had I stayed with her, mastered me for a moment. Deera leant forward and put her hand on my wrist. I relaxed, letting the heat dissipate and I shivered.

"Without what she did for you, you would be dead. Immolated, or through that portal, or something equally hideous. The control she gave you was the greatest gift, even for the price."

It was. We sat in silence for a few minutes. The condensation on the window slowly evaporated, and the others moved to one side of the lawns. Deera focused on the book.

"What I wouldn't give to speak to Foweller right now," she muttered, turning a page.

"Question." Church hobbled in. "Why not summon him. Why not summon all the spirits? Percival and your mother came here." He looked and sounded the same. Doubt gnawed.

Deera eyed him before speaking. "The essence of living creatures is tricky. Human spirits move on quickly if they endure at all. And even our kind who remain tends to do so only if they have cause."

His eyes flickered. "Unfinished business?"

"Or strong love, or duty, or tragedy. After the middle war, there was a great gathering of spirits. High Witches held a meeting and helped them move on. That'll be when we were last gathered like this." She kept staring at him.

"Okay, okay, fine. Deera, knower of things, who is he?" I pointed at Church.

She swallowed and dragged her stare away from him. She glanced at the others. After a minute while Church made himself coffee, tense and silent, she slumped back, running her finger over a page in the book. "Foweller talks about an 'anointed hope.' The seed of all power."

"I hope you don't think that's me." Church's eyes widened. He held everything back, still and guarded yet his hands trembled.

She stood and cupped his face as he came over, mug in hand. "And he shall appear, whole and beautiful, as made of light. He shall be love and kindness. He will fall and bleed for destiny."

He stepped back.

I stood, toppling my chair, and balling my fists. "You knew. That's why you saved him."

Deera put her hands up.

"Church, get our things. Are you going to stop us?" I asked Deera as Church backed out and went upstairs.

"That would be my job." Musa came in, sword and dagger in hand, and the others followed.

"He will not be sacrificed." I watched each face, the monster already raging inside me, stuttering into reality.

Everyone took a step away.

"We've been discussing your plan." Musa was easy calm.

Church barrelled down the stairs, chucked my coat to me, and I slid it on.

Musa inclined her head. "You can try to find out what you can about the Door and the demon you saw. Much of their focus will be on you, and it might be best if we weren't all together drawing attention. We thought we knew all the portals, and that we don't know this one terrifies me. Who's left from Witworth?"

"The children and young witches, and Lady Witworth and five of the council," Annabelle answered.

"Fine. You two need to draw attention away from us, so it's you they're focused on. We'll take a party to Witworth."

"What about the hunters?" asked Len.

"They're the least of our problems right now. With Estelle dead, her spells are lost, and her control over Adaline's power is gone. There's no stopping what's coming. We need to try to get in front of it."

"Then I gift you the book. Let's go."

Musa slid over the dagger, and for a moment my regret was keen, but there were things to be done.

We left the cottage out of reality behind.

DEEP IN THINE OWN SOUL, IS THE UGLY TRUTH

Church yawned and shifted in the passenger seat as we ate. "It's so quiet."

We'd parked at the top of a hill in the town closest to my mother's house and at the bottom were the solicitor offices that hired Church. Narrow Victorian streets wound around us in unnatural logic, and streetlamps blinked on, casting strange light. It was only two in the afternoon. There wasn't a soul to be seen.

"Yes." I looked around.

"You're angry?"

"The policy was bullshit, you say you're acting in good faith, and despite everything, I believe you."

"But you don't trust it?"

"Would you?"

He smiled bitterly. "No. Perhaps not. I'd never hurt you. I'm trying to take it all in, but... I know what you are and there is evil in the world." He squinted and swallowed, pain passing over his face. "If I'm part of it, I need to put it right. I need to know."

I held his hand, and he repressed the emotion that threatened to show itself.

"How long were we at Len's?"

Checking my phone, it'd been three days. "Time is funny." I tossed a wrapper into the carrier bag and sucked chocolate from my teeth. Constant hunger was irritating me.

The sky darkened further, and mist hovered. Condensation dripped off surfaces, and cold seeped everywhere.

The solicitor, Derek Fenwick, a middle-aged man, came out and hurried along the street. I got out and followed.

Church halted me and shivered. "Listen, stay out of sight, and let me see him alone. I know you're all powerful, but I'm quite good at my job, and you don't need to draw attention to yourself."

I eyed the rapidly disappearing man. "Are you really?"

"I got you to tell me what you are," Church smirked.

"That you did." I bit the inside of my cheek remembering that moment. "Does that come easy for you?"

"People like to tell me things."

I narrowed my eyes. "I'm sure they do." I got back in the car, watching him vanish. Threading everything together, the sense of inevitable hung over me, a pendulum about to swing. My spine crept, and I drank water. My stomach turned, still hungry.

I found my cigarettes and pulled one out. I'd not smoked a single one, and only lost a couple. A few were slightly battered from taking them out and putting them back in. An un-creased one between my two fingers lost a smattering of tobacco. I rolled it back and forth it for a minute, remembering the taste.

I checked the news. The death toll was steadily rising. Armies drafted, disposal programmes, state of emergency. It was definitely the end. My mind blanked, not quite able to grasp it, though I'd seen it.

A rumbling in the distance brought me around. I looked in the wing-mirror and an army ambulance roared past along with two trucks barely moving through the narrow streets.

Cars lined every possible spot with the owners inside hiding or dead. I resisted the impulse to panic as I watched one truck clip a bunch of cars.

"Rhere, where was that Door?" I thumped my head back.

"I have a phone you know."

I screamed, and put my hand to my heart. "Fuck's sake."

Rhere looked blankly at me as his head touched the top of the car.

"Also, how the fuck are you here?"

He looked all around him. "I'm not here. Nor are you. You touched my father the god, not only did it," he gestured with his hand to me as if trying to remember the word, "wake you up, it connected you to me."

"That's why I saw your memory." It wasn't a question, and I sighed, looking into the fog.

"You called me, but I like to text."

I laughed, and he grinned.

"You have questions?"

"Where was the Door you witnessed? Why didn't you stop it?"

"London, it was marshland then. And they built a temple to it, and then Romans came and built another temple, always with temples. Now?" He closed his eyes and drew breath. "I don't remember." He tilted his head. "Near the library entrance to me, the power of that glamour repels it, like magnets." He grinned so wide it looked odd.

"You're strange."

"But you like me anyway?" He kept the grin and leant over to me.

"Yes. You make me seem vaguely rational."

His smile dimmed, and he sat back. "I didn't know what they were at first. I was drawn to the power. There was a battle afterwards, I didn't know who was who. I watched. I have watched all unfold over time. I'm tired."

The endless glittering depth of his eyes welled with sorrow, and I reached out to him, but I was startled by the car door opening, making Rhere vanish in a second, and Church got in.

"What?"

"Nothing." I dug some gum out of my coat and offered him some.

"Is there anything you don't have in that coat?"

I put my thoughts of Rhere aside and focused. "I don't even know anymore. What did he say?"

Church took a piece and huffed, letting his head fall back against the headrest before taking out his phone. He fiddled with it for a moment and set it on the dash.

The recording was muffled with the sound of his coat, but their voices were clear.

"Have you found her?"

"No."

There was a pause and movement. I sat forward.

"The insurance company needs to know."

"What's the urgency? Everyone is sick anyway."

"It's not just them, the police are involved, what with the fire at Witworth. You said it was before you could go there?"

"Yeah, I'm still chasing up her associates. But something feels off about the whole thing. From my understanding, it was not a good place."

"That might be so." There was a long pause. "Don't search for things that don't concern you, you know what we need."

"Did you know Estelle?"

There was a sharp breath. "Why?"

"Curiosity, seeing as Miss Greyling is connected to the same place her mother was, I'm interested in any other connections."

"I knew her a little. Strange woman. Very short. Odd. We humoured her. Could be quite difficult."

"Hmm. From what I've figured she had no income, and I wonder where the money came to pay for things. In case that's where Miss Greyling has gone."

"I don't know. Now, I've got to get on. This flu outbreak means everywhere is operating at half measures, so I'm swamped."

Brief goodbyes followed, and Church turned off the recorder.

"He knows. He's part of it."

Church pocketed his phone. "He does. Looked cagey and uncomfortable when I asked about the money. Normally, I go in with a docket and go through whatever I'm looking into. He didn't ask me where it was or why I'd not found anything."

"Who is he working for. Witworth? Hunters? Why this charade with a policy? Because at this point, I don't think it's a coincidence. Someone brought you to me for a purpose. My connection to you, everything that's happened, no, there's more here than merely finding me. But here's the weirdest thing. There's a massive pandemic, and he's all nonchalant not giving a shit. What mortal doesn't give a shit about something like that?"

"One who's sure he won't get sick."

He smiled, and we set off. I glanced in the mirror half-expecting to see Rhere sitting in the back, but there was nothing other than a quiet, misty street.

We stayed in a B&B, a quaint old brick place with doilies and twee prints of animals on every wall. The old woman in charge violently coughed as we took the key. I watched her for a minute.

"It's this blasted mist." She croaked in a laugh.

Church and I looked at each other.

In the room, I stood against the tepid radiator and looked out. "Is everyone completely oblivious?"

"Apparently. What are you thinking?"

I nearly told him about Rhere, but I think he had enough to process without demigods from other realities. "When we first met, something was off about the cottage, but not just that. This place. All of it. Feels like... not glamour but under an influence of something."

Church moved around, but I didn't turn.

"Are you afraid of me now?"

"No." I turned then.

"We haven't really talked. I don't understand any of it but what I feel is real." He nudged the obnoxiously patterned rug with his ruined shoe. I needed to comfort and love him. I blinked and gripped the sill.

He stilled and approached me slowly. "I was dead. But you were this pure light, and it was so beautiful. It felt like I'd gone home."

I couldn't look away from him.

"I'm afraid." He lowered his face, mouth twisted in pain.

"So am I." I cupped his face.

A few tears fell, and I dashed them away.

"Make me forget. Just for a while. Anchor me." The tremble in his voice broke any resolve I had. I grabbed his shirt and kissed him. He was all need and desire as we fell on the bed. I laughed as he kissed down my neck, and I undressed him.

"Are you in pain?" I pushed his shirt off.

"A little. I need to feel, take me, hurt me." He grazed his teeth along my skin.

Our connection overrode all doubt. And for that alone, I didn't trust it. Some tactic or device of Witworth, but I could not deny it or him, no matter what. The compulsion was too strong.

I took care of him, soothed his need and desire as he soothed mine. I lay over him after, staring in the dark. I ran my fingers over the bruises from his healing wound as well as the marks I made. As I looked at him, chin propped on his chest, my heart ached.

My soul screamed *Protect him at all costs*, and to do that I needed to stop the solicitor. Careful not to wake him, I dressed, pulling on whatever was nearest, including Church's white shirt. I smelt the collar and grinned to myself, slipping my coat on. With my dagger at the ready, I went out.

A grandfather clock struck twelve as I reached the dated hall. I swallowed all the saliva in my mouth, my stomach turning, and went out into a bitter night.

Everything was thick with rime, and the fog hung low. It was a glamour of sorts. I stopped, turning, making the green tinged air turn around me.

The dark whispered to me, warning me away. I laughed. The air clung to me, trying to slow my step, and I knew I was on the right path. It felt connected somehow.

The hissing man that came through the Door felt with me as I pushed through the whispering mist. To mortal ears, it might have been no more than the wind, but I heard it, spanning distance and time.

I couldn't see much, but moving along the deserted streets, I passed an emergency medical station set up at a school — though it was shut up with rubbish and vehicles abandoned all about — and found my way to the office. I broke in with a good shove to the door.

I went through the office and found nothing. The filing cabinets were empty, desk bare, nothing. No sign it was a business. I sat in the office chair, swinging side to side.

A painting on a woodchip wall caught my eye. Abstract daubs of thick bright paint seemed familiar, and an odd choice for the office. Lifting the frame, I found a hole behind it.

Inside was a lockbox, and after forcing it, I found a small leather diary filled with numbers and letters; a code I didn't know and pocketed it. The only other thing there was the rental agreement, so I decided to visit the billing address, but I needed to make another stop first.

It wasn't that far to Church's office.

Inside, I remembered my meeting with him with warmth. His filing cabinets were mostly empty. One or two things. I had my own drawer.

The policy agreement looked legit, as did the insurer.

The detritus of human existence is in its things. He had nothing. No plants. One mug. A printed certificate of some qualification I hadn't heard of. Playing at having a life. His work was perfunctory. All surface. I was sure he believed in who he was but whether that was real? I wasn't convinced. Enemy or lover didn't really matter anymore though. I had to keep him with me.

Leaving, I put my doubts aside and went to find Fenwick.

He lived in a large house nestled behind trees at the edge of the town. Double garage with a host of cars parked out front, gated, and a separate building off to the side. The definition of 'did well and shows it in gauche display.'

I broke in, the alarm pipping as I went upstairs, and thick carpet kept my footfall silent.

His wife slept in a separate bedroom. I squatted over her just as the alarm went off, and as she came around, I put my hand over her mouth.

She struggled, and I put my finger to my lips. Mr Fenwick shouted and ran in. The screeching was unpleasant, and I turned back to him and grimaced.

He looked unsurprised. I tasted the woman's fear beneath me, I knew her greed and avarice and felt the delight she took in cruelty. She was vile. As bad as the man in the doorway.

"Turn it off." I squeezed the woman's neck.

He nodded and did as I demanded, returning in the quiet. The woman struggled the whole time.

"You wanted to find me?" I took my dagger and held it to her throat, rendering her compliant.

It was easy to know her truth. It hit me then; I didn't get that from Church.

"What do you want?" I sniffed the air, finding him not entirely human.

The smug arrogance of Fenwick revolted me. "To take my rightful place. For you to be on the winning side, Miss Greyling."

The wife couldn't breathe. I saw the things she did with her husband watching, and pain she caused. The viciousness of her. Nothing preternatural, no demon in her blood. Just average deplorable human evil.

He was blank. I got nothing from him but the foulness of corrupted bodies. My hand warmed and the air heated.

"We're on your side."

"My side? And who's we?" My demon was quiet, watching events with interest. The wife tried to pull my arm away. I was steel to her.

Her fear grew to a panicked crescendo. I smiled. Fenwick's face fell.

"All right, another question."

He nodded.

From my pocket, I pulled the diary and held it up before putting it back. "What's that?"

His eyes fixed on it. "Jobs I get from my employer. I pass them on."

I pressed the knife, and the woman whimpered.

"Watch your kind. Find them." He put his hands up.

"Who's your employer?"

When he didn't speak, I drew blood.

"You'll have to kill me." He dropped his hands.

"What about her? Do I have to kill her too?" I tilted my head.

He was silent, watching his wife struggle beneath me. I hated humans; I really did. My shadow laughed, filled my limbs, crooning.

"There's something very bad about to happen to you, Mr Fenwick. It's going to be horrific. One chance. Who took out the policy or was it merely fabricated?"

I sneered, fighting for control, and the heat ignited sparks of dust around us as the air grew hot and dry.

Fenwick shook his head, sweat steaming off him. "But, you're the one. The chosen Doomer. The strongest."

"Now Fenwick." The sensation of heat filtering through me was orgasmic. Seductive. How easy to fall to it. Let my friend out to play. I pressed down harder on the woman, who held her breath.

Fenwick pissed himself. "I cannot tell you. I'm bound." He cried.

"Is it to do with the hunters?"

No answer. The curtains caught fire.

"The Door in London?"

He struggled for breath.

I couldn't hold back. There was no time for a potion. No, I had no inclination to take one.

Beneath me, wife wailed, fire took the bedding, and I let her go. The room started to burn, the flame leaping across the carpet. I could've stopped it. I did nothing and watched him become a squealing wall of flame.

I opened the window, dropped out and let the place burn to the ground. My brain and body rushed with the high. The power and tingling remnant of warmth, like a good whisky and a joint after sex.

Half-grinning with easy strides, I made my way back to Church, and there was no whispering in the air, only held breath.

Church slept so peacefully as I let myself in the room.

"I did something."

He sat up, rubbing his eyes. I sat on the windowsill just as the sun rose.

"What."

"I might have killed Fenwick."

"Fucking hell." He lay back.

"He was a corrupt human, and his wife was a monster, albeit a human one. Interesting thing. Look outside."

He got up, and I tried not to admire his glorious naked body. The fog had almost gone along with the strange glamour it cast over the town. The place felt abandoned and decaying.

"Shit."

"He worked for someone who asked him to find me."

"Shit." He dressed in fresh clothes from his bag. He slipped on a clean but rumpled shirt.

"Do you own anything other than white shirts? Do you have trainers, sweats, anything?"

He paused. "Come to think of it, no. Is that strange?"

"We have to go to London. The unknown Door is there, and Fenwick had this." I passed Church the diary.

He turned down his mouth as he flicked through it. "There's an address. A club."

"Helwent. It's a rich boy's thing."

"While we're here, we should go to the cottage."

"Why, there's nothing there." I narrowed my eyes.

He nodded and handed the book back.

"Why do you want to go?" I pinned him with a sharp look before stripping and washing at the sink.

"It feels like you should be there for something."

I patted my face and underarms with the thin pink towel. "We're spinning a lot of plates, and time isn't our friend. I need to know about that portal. The Court hasn't given us a lot of rope here, but depending how things go, we can come back."

"Then let's go."

When we left, the woman who'd been at reception was sprawled on the floor, dead.

I leant over her. Not mortal illness. Blood dried at her mouth and on her hanky. Crust at her eyes. I gagged on the smell.

"Fuck." Church went pale, and I grabbed him, dragging him out.

I ferreted out my hand sanitiser and passed it over.

We headed south and raced all the way. Though a few roads were blocked with cars, the motorways were mostly empty.

△ △ △

With a shiver, a bead of sweat rolled down my back. In dim light, as we navigated the city, I was lost in a dream I couldn't hold onto. Birds clung onto powerlines, preparing to migrate, and the sound of the place was quiet. There did seem to be a lot of birds. The day faded, but it wasn't yet noon. The sun sank into gloomy urban sprawl, the birds lifted into the air, and my skin goosed.

"Where am I going?"

Scrubbing my face, I thought. I rented a small studio in a rundown Victorian tenement a few miles away but couldn't go back to it now, not that it was a loss; I kept nothing of value there. I guided him to a place witches used when they visited. Though there was little moving traffic, some roads were clogged with cars, but we eventually made our way around. No-one was there when we arrived. I expected it to be brimming. After showers, I made coffee, and we ate instant noodles.

"What now?"

I hadn't thought that far.

OH, PRECIOUS FAITH, HOW I MISS THEE

wanted to go look for Helwent first, but something about Church's face made me hesitate. "What is it?"

"When you were in the shower, I looked at the diary again."

I shoved more noodles in my mouth from my second bowl.

"There's an address."

I paused midchew, and he slid it over.

His brow furrowed. "I've seen it before, but I can't think why it's important. I was looking for a missing boy, I think, I can't recall. Why can't I remember?"

I swallowed. "This is a hunter place, and I'd been watching them for a year. They were just men once, an irritation, but easily managed. Then a year ago, it changed. They took power from somewhere. The thing that attacked me outside your office was one. I was supposed to find out why and how their agenda changed. I got nowhere, but this place I knew. It's like a safe house."

He stared at it. "I need answers."

"Okay, we'll go look, see what's happening."

We did.

Church scowled as water dripped onto his head where he sheltered under a hawthorn tree. Drizzle hung in the air, still misty. The darkness of the day deepened, but it wasn't even five.

"I get the feeling something is off."

"The last time you said that you died."

He smirked and looked back across the park.

On the other side of the railings was the Georgian townhouse that I spent a week watching, baiting them to figure their habits and patterns when their behaviour became bolder months ago.

They used the place like a stage post inn, coming and going constantly in a procession of the same crap suits and bland hair. It was too clean and tidy. Too everything. Jarring against the neglected cityscape in the grip of a flu pandemic.

A few people went about their business but not many. More rubbish than usual banked up against bins, stinking in the wet air, and a man wove through the bags.

"There."

It was cold, and Church stamped his feet with his lovely handmade shoes still scuffed and creased with mud. Squinting, he followed my gaze. "I see him." He pushed off, and I stayed a few paces behind.

With his hands in his pockets, he approached the clean-cut man in a high street suit, smiling. "Hi."

The man, as remarkably pasty and uninteresting as every other hunter I'd come across, puffed himself up.

Circling so I approached from behind, I grabbed the man in a headlock and dragged him down a side path. Church made sure nobody noticed and followed, not that there was anyone about.

The man bared his teeth and fought me.

"Listen, if you want to fight, we can, but you'll die like all the others." I looked deep into his bland mediocrity, and I saw how weak he was, how manipulated and moulded into committing heinous acts.

He went lax, staring back, lost. I wondered how he saw me. How terrifying I was to him. "What do you want?"

"To be merciful." I squeezed his throat a little and let him go, keeping him crowded in a corner.

Church sniffed in the cold. "Have you heard of Derek Fenwick?"

"Solicitor? Yes." The hunter didn't take his eyes off me as he felt his neck.

"What does he do for you?"

"Tells us where you are, makes sure we're paid, you know, day to day stuff." He glanced at Church. "Why?"

"Did you ever hear of Estelle Greyling? Lived up north." I narrowed my eyes.

"Yeah, the head witch, we've been watching her for months. Nearly a year."

I bit the inside of my cheek trying not to laugh in surprise.

Church stepped a little closer. "A year?"

"Well, yeah, we had new management, and how we worked changed. We've had real missions."

"Who's in charge?"

The man deflated. "Lord Deltonly. He's got money and connections. Fenwick is on his team. They approached us. Before, we mostly reacted to things, documented them in the records. Now we act."

Neither Church nor I spoke but glanced at each other.

"We've got instruction of witches to kill, all but one. The High Witch's daughter."

I raised my brows. "Go on."

"We had to watch her only, she's important, and the key to stopping the evil. Not everyone agreed. A faction broke away. Tried to kill her. Everyone who goes after her disappears." As he stared at me, his words slowed, as if understanding slowly dawned over him.

"You're a pawn in a game, the rules of which you don't know. If I were you, I'd find a comfortable hole because we're all going to die."

He swallowed and slid along the blackened brick as I let him go.

"He'll talk."

"I know." At the end of the alleyway, I watched him hurry along. We kept our distance.

"Who's this Lord?"

I did a quick search on my phone. "Barnaby Pentworthy-James." His image flashed up on the screen, and all my breath left me. "Fuck me. It's the man I saw go through the unknown Door."

"What?"

We picked up our pace as I read from my phone.

"It's perfect, really. Took the title a year ago after his father's death. A year. Imagine that."

Church huffed, pulling me along to keep up.

I found a Reddit thread. "Huh, this gets weirder. He belongs to the Helwent Street Gentlemen's club, a mysterious place, full of rumours. Titles are hereditary. Rumour of unnatural activity. Death and disappearances. Ghosts." I halted, putting my phone away. "The Door is in the club. The address, Helwent Street, is near the library entrance to Rhere's. Shit. It opens and takes the ripe fruit of the newly anointed Lord. Massive resources. In the right position, the demon tapped into power already there. Fuck."

The man halted, looking panicked as he tried a locked door. We hung back.

Church leant on the wall opposite me. "Barnaby Pentworthy, or whatever his name is, takes his seat in the Lords, sets up watch on your mother because, I assume, he can't find you. He uses the hunters to do the job, Fenwick was one? Anyway, they bide their time, knowing they need you. Your mother dies. You go. I'm employed to find you. Stay close. Things begin."

I wasn't sure that was all of it.

"I knew him. In the vision, I knew him. His, his grief and loneliness. Felt like I was part of his life. He didn't want to kill me. Everyone wants me dead."

Church shrugged his mouth down.

Our target headed into the nearest tube. The cold smell of musty underground hit me as we travelled down the escalator, and the dry wind and noise normally mitigated by people felt louder. There were too few people for the usually busy station.

The man turned onto a deserted platform. We hung back, me in front. 'Cancelled due to driver shortage' flashed on the train display.

The man turned back. We ducked onto the opposite platform and followed him back up and out. We'd sailed through open barriers with no staff in sight.

"Do you think I'm a pawn?" Church asked a little breathless.

"I don't know what you are, but it doesn't matter. You make me feel different." I slowed my step. "I feel."

Church grabbed my arm, searching my eyes. "I..." He smiled, blushing a little.

We stared at each other, and I caressed his face, stubble rough.

I wanted to say so much, all new and unnerving. Instead, I nuzzled his cheek for a second. "We can't lose him."

Church cleared his throat and took my hand with a firm grip, and we hurried on. The moment fading as we saw more horror with every step.

Every so often, we passed manic temp hospitals, soldiers in hazmat suits, army trucks stationed with supplies next to others being filled with body bags.

The one hospital we did see was blocked off with cars haphazardly parked around ambulances, though we saw no-one moving around. The scent of human decay in the air.

Church and I glanced at each other, still holding hands. The quiet was oppressive, and there was only us. The man headed into a building after an hour's walk.

"We should break in."

Church was pale, and I grabbed his coat and held him by the lapels. "Okay?"

He put his hands on my waist, staring into my eyes. "You make me feel too. It's like I've woken up for the first time."

I kissed him briefly and grinned. "Ready to fuck shit up?"

"Yes."

△ △ △

Zealots are dangerous. Anything that requires unquestioning devotion is a lousy idea and looking at the players of this game, all manoeuvring for vantage and power, nauseated me.

With a steady breath, I focused on the neat little building that looked like a Victorian schoolhouse nestled behind oaks that our new friend went in. The rain had stopped, but the damp cold was everywhere.

"What now?"

"We break in." I turned my cigarettes over in my hand, itching for one.

Around the back, where a children's park backed onto the building, was a tall spiked fence. No cameras that we saw, or any other security measures, so we jumped it.

Keeping low, the mist that hovered shielded us, and we crept to the back, listening. The door was unlocked. Empty and silent halls greeted us.

"This screams trap," Church whispered.

"I know. Ready?"

"Not really."

Edging in, we saw a man pass the end of the far corridor with a stack of books and followed him. He descended a staircase, and it seemed to be just him.

We blocked the stairs, and when he spotted us, he sat in the nearest seat. He was old, white hair, papery pink skin, and rheumy eyes. He took off his glasses and set them down. "I knew you'd come." The man wasn't looking at me. "The end has begun." He gave the air of all-knowing importance.

"You know who I am?" Unimpressed, I walked over and sat opposite.

"You're the last Doomer. Daughter of Estelle. We've been thwarting the endeavours of evil and magic for centuries, and for every victory, there's a loss, and now you sully our walls. A week ago, you'd already be dead." He seemed grieved, not angry.

"Would you like some truth? Witches are not evil. We're ordained to fight that which lives beyond the realm portals. Hunters seem to have confused the matter."

His deeply wrinkled brow furrowed further before he looked at Church.

"Who is he?" I pointed at him. I was sick of the question.

"I believe that is Edward Church." The old man lifted his chin up.

"What part do I play?" Church stepped forward.

The old man smiled. "Oh, you can stop what comes." He nodded at me. "You're not the only ones with power."

Church vibrated with anger, his skin flushed, and he grabbed the man by the lapels, pulling him out the chair. "Who am I?"

As Church's frustration finally bubbled over, I smirked, watching the display.

The old man's mouth flapped, seeing something I didn't. "Lord God save us."

The tension hung between them, and I looked from one to the other. "What do you see, old man?"

A tear fell from his rheumy eyes. "Evil."

"Your God is a fool." Church threw him back into his seat.

I smiled at Church, and he steadied himself, straightening his shirt and hair, reining it all back in. I tapped the table with my knuckle. "Mr Church is not evil. He's one of the few people who isn't. What makes you say he is?"

Shaking, he put his hand to his chest. "Evil comes in many vessels. The agents of the devil come in disguise."

"Oh good grief." I pinched the bridge of my nose. "This is a waste of time if you can't give me a straight answer. Fenwick."

"Came to us with prophecies, proof of unnatural occurrences. The end times were coming, and with it, he brought a weapon." Shame cut his voice.

"You think we're monsters but we're not. You started killing us to take our power."

His eye twitched, and hands trembled. "Yes. Everything changed. Some rebelled, but others became fanatics of the new way. Addicted to the power offered. Then... this sickness, plague, has come, and it is too late."

"You're right it is but not because of us."

With that, three men in latex gloves and face masks barrelled down the stairs, and I stood.

"One move and I burn it all." Heat rippled in my skin and muscle, making the air kindle, dust burning in the air. In a flash, a book caught, and the old man put it out.

"All your precious history lost. Your lives over. All of it gone. Ashen waste. Choose wisely." My companion woke.

The old man flicked his wrist, and the others backed off Church. "You think we were wrong."

"I know it. You work for the demons you despise and don't have the first idea of the consequences of your actions. Insipid arrogance."

With a sneer, he lifted his chin. "You've brought this sickness. Our men are dead. You must die to end it."

"Then why was I protected and watched only?" I leant down to him, and he shrivelled. "You hide and see nothing. All this time and you've achieved death. You've aided the true enemy. The end of the world began a year ago with your employer."

He gaped as we pushed past the hunters, and they let us go.

"It really is too late." I halted on what should have been a busy street passing abandoned cars and shuttered shops. We made our way back to the safe house in silence, weighted down with it.

Church held my hand, pensive, his long legs striding back through the quiet city.

I slipped my coat off as we got in. "Now what?"

He took a deep breath, staring at nothing.

"What is it?"

"I don't understand what this is." He looked at his hands. "What am I?" The pain in his eyes hurt my heart.

I pushed his coat off. "I taste evil and corruption. It reeks, and there's not the smallest bit of it in you. You're the opposite. You're beautiful, alive, and we're together. Right now, that's all there is. You're right; terrible things are happening. So we need to make the most of the little things we have. I don't understand our connection, but we have it. I feel it." I put his large, warm hand on my heart, and the pain lessened.

His jaw set, gaze hard, and he dug his fingers into my scalp and kissed me. We stumbled through the house, stripping each other until we fell naked into the bedroom without quite making it to the bed.

BUT WHAT GRIEF REFLECTS INTO MY SOUR BONES

As the sun rose, I lay over Church who had bite marks on his hips, and I put them there. I'd dreamt of this Barnaby person. His face appeared in a towering crystal chasm, and we were side by side. I held onto the images in a pink dawn. The world was utterly silent.

"I need to go look at Helwent."

"Alone?" Church held me tighter.

"Alone would be best."

He cupped my face. Without speaking, he stared, eyes searching and a soft smile.

"What?" I held his hand to my face.

"A lot has happened. Just taking it in."

"Are you now?"

Pressing him back, I kissed him. I only wore my jumper, and he pulled it off, kissing my shoulder.

"We have things to do." I pushed off him and got out of bed.

Church scrunched his eyes up. "I'm afraid of what it means, Adaline. What should I do?"

I found my clothes and started dressing while he watched.

"Stay safe. You have a part in this. The hunters are useless men who are so deep in lies and mistruths, we can learn nothing from them. It's a dead end. You were used by them for something, but I know when we met the urge to keep you safe was all important." The way he looked at me made me bite my lip.

Crawling to the end of the bed, he swallowed and snatched my top from my hands. "I need you." He kissed me as I laughed, the warmth in my throat turning into a moan.

I pulled at his hair as he manoeuvred me under him. Nothing quite like the end of the world, dying, and metaphysical questions to stimulate sexual appetite.

He nipped down my neck to my breast, pressing his teeth over the fabric of my bra.

I needed to go, but his touch was too delicious. I pushed him back, and he smirked. Like this he was raw; his polite veneer gone. I'd never know this again. Who knew what horrors waited. This good, brief thing gave me strength.

I let my bra fall. "Resume."

"Teeth?"

"Teeth."

He kissed me hard, and I caressed him all over, feeling out his flesh. Mapping his muscles and sweet softness.

He bit my shoulder and urged me down, speaking between kisses and nibbles. "Last time you were in charge."

"And you want to show me what you've got?"

"Yes." He closed his mouth over my breast and sank his teeth in. I cried out at the sharp bite and aching draw in my flesh, my nerves pulsed, and I pressed closer to him, locking my legs around his waist, binding us together.

He was a flurry of lust and movement, exploring my body, showing me a thread of him I hadn't expected.

Kneeling up, he pulled off my jeans, making me laugh. Flipping me over, he muttered something before biting an arse cheek, slowly increasing pressure. I cried out, relishing the sharp pain.

"I want you." I almost didn't recognise his gruff voice.

"Yes."

Pulling my hips up, he entered me. My vision stuttered, the darkness hovering in the corner of my being. The thing in my soul, in my bones and flesh, relished being fucked. I relished it. Pleasure hummed and I was losing the line between where I began and the thing I was tethered to ended.

Even as I came, pushing back against his hips, I was afraid of myself. Of who I was becoming. It writhed and came with me, knowing infinite pleasure. I saw it, and it saw me; both awake and needy. I became an animal and gloried.

Church came unabashed. Panting hard, he ran his hand along my spine. "Fuck. Sorry."

"Are you? What for?"

"Well, I'm not, but I um... I don't know."

Laughing, I pulled off him and turned over. Red-cheeked and sheepish, he fell onto to me, and I held so tight.

"What is it?" he mumbled into my hair.

"You. This. I want to hold onto this moment."

"I died." He leant up on his elbows. "Died. I know what waits now. I'm not afraid of it, but I'm terrified of what it means, what all this means. Why it is and my part in it."

"I wish I could say it'll be okay. We'll figure this out."

"What if I'm not human?"

"Well, I'm not, so that's fine."

He laughed as we lay for a moment and sobered. "It never occurred to me before now, but we've not used protection at all."

"We don't get sick. We look human, but we're not. We live long lives, though most of us die in the fight. I don't know if we were once human and evolved or made to pass as human."

"What about pregnancy?" He flushed.

I sat up and went to the bathroom. When I came back, I started dressing. Church hadn't moved, though his brow furrowed.

"It's not easy for us to bear children and only with other witches that I know of." I paused, not facing him. "Mother told me what might happen and what happened to her. I am the end, or I facilitate the end by enduring what she did. When I was nineteen, I decided that I would never to allow myself to carry a child. I don't have a uterus now." I didn't look at him.

"I'm sorry."

"Don't be. I'm not." I wasn't, but it wasn't easy to say aloud, and no-one knew. "It wasn't a noble gesture for humanity's sake. They wanted us to be pure and fertile should we be called. Fuck that. Knowing what mother went through, I couldn't allow it to happen. I fucked everyone I could. When I burnt Witworth, they told me it was time. I'd go in the Door and come out pregnant. Before they do it, they'd check and poke me, and they'd know I couldn't. Living under this weight made me a certain way. I had to be. I didn't care about anything other than me." I stared at him, not knowing how to explain the change in these last days. "I'd have ripped a hole in myself and anyone in my way to do something. Now, I feel differently." I finished dressing.

He lay on the bed, half wrapped in a sheet. As I slipped on my coat, he sat up, giving me a delightful image of his body. "I'm sorry. I can't imagine how afraid you've been all your life. Screaming in silence at who you are. So much pressure. But you're a good person and haven't an inkling how extraordinary you are. Adaline, be safe. For me."

I swallowed hard. "You too. And if not, haunt me."

We stared at each other for a minute, and with increasing dread, I feared I'd never see him again.

I kissed him once, no more than a firm press of lips, but he held my hair, bunched between his fingers, our mouths close.

"I love you," I said it hurried and rushed, and it wasn't a thing I thought I'd ever say, but I did. In all the world, and though I didn't know him, he was mine, and I loved him.

I hurried away, and as I opened the door, he said it. "I love you too."

I let it close softly behind me.

CONSPIRE AGAINST THE ENEMY, MY FRIEND

Helwent Street club was posh, and a place where I'd be noticed. It was hard to push Church aside in my mind, but he was too distracting and lovely. I kept hearing him say he loved me. I half-laughed, not quite rationalising it. Shaking it off, I focused.

The stench of wealth and entitlement was everywhere, and as the same foggy weather stagnated, I turned up my collar to the cold with my eyes on the quiet gentlemen's club. The silence was starting to jar, and I pulled out my phone.

Nothing new. Outlets had stopped posting news. There was nothing. I swallowed thickly against the dread. I stared for too long at the broken screen, looking for anything.

A few army vehicles were stationed at abandoned check points. A few people in white protective clothing moved like ghosts through the streets, but other than that, there was nothing and no-one. I couldn't process it.

As I was considering the best course to break in, a car pulled up in front of the Helwent gentleman's club and there he was, the man from my vision. He sniffed the air, and I receded. In he went.

The driver pulled down a side street, and unsheathing my dagger, I followed. My body vibrated. A strange shuddering desire ran through me. The Door was inside, I felt it. I wanted to screech into the air and signal the failure of humanity.

Nearly stumbling, I focused.

I tapped on the window of the car and startled the driver. As the window slid down, I put the dagger into his gaping mouth. He stank.

If I killed him, Barnaby would know, but if I let him live, he'd know. "Out you get, sunshine."

There was a vacancy in him, whoever he was had long checked out. Its sourness wafted, and waxy skin had cracked in places.

I dropped my hand. It looked pitiful.

"What's your boss doing?"

It squelched a noise, hissed and lunged at me.

I immolated him in seconds behind the overflowing trolley bins. It writhed and squealed, and I dodged as it flailed before it fell in a heap. It left nothing but a dirty stain behind. A phone rang from inside the car. I looked through it, ignoring the incoming call from 'Boss'. I checked the open apps, and the address list of destinations included a nice house on the other side of London. "You're kidding me." I tossed it on the seat and made my way across town. That was too easy.

I hated the deserted city, the smell of sickness and death pervaded, yet I passed an open shop.

Ducking in, the shelves were bare. A small elderly woman wheezed at the counter. Curious, I bought one of the few cans of pop left and several bars of chocolate.

"All right?"

She lifted her grey face to me, not quite understanding me. I put all the coins I had on the counter and left.

I ate on the way, shivering and starved.

When I reached his house, secluded and gated, it imposed over me. Another house, separated by a wall and gardens, backed onto it and was less fortified. I strolled past as the faint smell of decay wafted out. I followed it, recoiling at the scent.

The sweet foulness was cloying but was not mortal death; it tasted like a demon. I rang Len.

"We wondered how you were."

"Hunters are a dead end, but they work for the demon, how apt. We found the Door. And the demon. Look, do you know this pandemic isn't like previous ones?"

"We think Witworth is already open." Len sounded like he was moving around. "The Court is already gearing up. A lot of people have left cities, staying inside, apparently there were measures in place to handle a pandemic on this scale. There's nothing any of us can do now but close the portal."

"I burnt the Manor down. I set this in motion." The weight of what I'd done squeezed me tight, and I couldn't breathe. I fell to my knees, eyes straining, and heat dried the air. It took every ounce of strength not to ignite everything in a fifty-foot radius. Even as it smoked, I screamed with the effort.

They were right; I was the coming death.

I picked up my phone when I heard Len talking, sweat pissing out of me.

"Listen. This was always their plan. With the Witworth Door comes death. Its occupant's goal was the destruction of humanity so they can inhabit this reality. There is only us and them. They will come and feast on the dead. They will devour the fabric of this existence so they can be in their true state. This was inevitable. We saw it and was always the purpose of the portals. To bring the end of all things. Adaline, it's up to us; there's no-one else. Focus on Helwent while we deal with Witworth."

Closing my eyes, I put my hand over my mouth. I let despair crash and pulled it back. Something turned off in me at the peak; a numb response and its familiar ease gave me strength. I truly was a Doom Baby; born of the Door.

Wiping the few tears that escaped, I sat up, still and calm. Adaline was a monster, and I had to remain as that.

I had a plan. I was going to destroy it all. Every Door and demon.

Breaking into the house via a sash window, I sat in Barnaby's study, drinking his aged brandy from a heavy crystal glass. The room smelt of leather and wealth, and something alluring like a memory. Comfortable.

In a desk drawer was a black leather diary with thick vellum pages filled with strange yet familiar sketches and symbols scratched in blood. In other places, spidery handwriting that I barely made out talked of Witworth.

We've waited so long, my love, and I cannot wait to hold you. I will serve my lord, my master, and give myself to you. The sense of longing made me ache. I wanted to weep and closed the volume carefully, running my hand over the cover.

Slipping it into my pocket, I finished my drink and made myself comfortable by the unlit fire. Prepared. With purpose.

Later, as the day darkened and cast me in shadow, I heard him return. My mind had been elsewhere, but I didn't remember what I was thinking about.

Barnaby came into the study, and I knew he was not human, and weirdly, I wanted to throw myself at him.

I ignited the fire with a thought, and he glanced wordlessly at it, before sitting in the opposite chair.

He was handsome, unnaturally so. Slick black hair, ashen skin, large dark eyes that were too much like mine. He scrutinised me, peering deep into my body and soul. I didn't like it and picked up my glass. He smirked.

He crossed his legs and slid the tie from his collar. "You didn't need to kill my driver, I had to walk back. I only expected you to beat him until he talked, which he would have, easily. So, you're the Witworth bitch."

"I am." The other side of me preened and made my body pulse.

"I've been waiting." He raised his arched brows briefly and shook his foot. Next to him was a small circular table with a glass dish on it, and a business card caught my eye. Black with gold writing.

"And you're in my house because?" He turned his hands palm up, and I imagined them on me.

"What was it like? When you stepped through."

He swallowed. "You're assuming that I'm the mortal soul. You shouldn't. That pathetic man is truly gone."

"You're that which existed before?"

He grinned, but I didn't like it. "And you, daughter bastard creation, are not going to stop what's coming."

"Is that so?" From within, I called to Barnaby in a feral cry, and its need raged. Shifting my vision, I held onto Church and his love.

Barnaby saw it, his lips parting, eyes on my mouth for a minute too long. "Where's the child?"

I didn't move or ask.

"You don't know, do you?" He laughed and bit his lip. "How perfect. We've been searching for Estelle's ward for months, and I was sure you knew. Adaline, keeper of secrets." Barnaby gave me a perfectly hideous smile.

Ward? I put it together. The solicitor and town, the glamour, watching my mother, hunting for Doomers. Church. "You used the hunters?"

"Oh that." He stood, poured himself a drink and sat again but wouldn't look away from me.

I kept seeing images of us entwined and whole. I licked my lips.

"It seemed strategic. Aren't they adorable? They're so occupied under misdirection and made finding your kind so much easier."

"The investigator? In your employ too?"

"He came into my radar via Fenwick, and I assume it was you who immolated him, how tastefully dramatic. Not that he's required now because..." he looked me over. "This investigator person is with you a lot. You seem to have taken to him, but I wouldn't trust him, there's something not quite right with blondie, isn't there?" He said it with disdain.

I opened my mouth to speak, but nothing came out.

"If you give me the child, I'll let you keep your pet." With a playful glint, he drank his brandy.

As much as I wanted to ask him what child, I held onto the deadness in my heart and stayed steady in silence.

He licked his lips, and I imagined how the drink tasted on them. The cut of alcohol, sweetness and him. I tried not to squirm as he spoke.

"I had a dream recently, and you were at the club. Did you have a vision? The truth within you is seeking to be free. Let me show you." His cadence was too quick and un-paced, words bent in a sharp voice. Everything about him upended me, and the room spun. He stood, slipping off his impeccably tailored jacket. The action was seductive, precise, showing his beauty. My mouth watered as warm firelight softened him.

In easy slowness, he moved closer and straddled my lap, and iron thighs pinned me in the chair. He put his hands to my throat, and I smiled when he squeezed lightly; the lust overwhelming.

"I see it," he hissed, mouth near mine, "your demon. I've waited for you in time beyond knowledge."

My creature writhed in my flesh for him. I moaned.

Desire filtered unbidden, and I revolted. Had I been human, there'd be no fighting it, and Barnaby couldn't anticipate that. Ego and arrogance rolled off every decision, and that assumption was his undoing.

I rubbed my face along his, and let my dagger slide out of my sleeve, even as my spirit flickered.

"Yes." I pressed my hips up to him, and the pleasure of finally being together filled my heart.

"You can be free; we can take it all. Everything is primed. Ready. I see you." He undulated over me, and I adjusted my grip on the blade. "The others are in place. We can take this world."

"Thank you," I whispered, "for telling me everything I needed to know."

He paused, lips brushing mine with electric energy arousing me so strongly I couldn't see, but in a single swift motion, I stabbed Barnaby in the kidney.

His mouth widened, he went rigid, and I screamed. Unbound grief poured through me.

"You think I'm that easy to kill." He growled, squeezing my neck harder.

"Do you think I used a mortal blade?" I pulled it out and stabbed him repeatedly until he fell off me, and I sat on his chest, squatting like the monster I am.

I knew his pain, I felt it in my marrow. I cried. Blood lined his lips, and he scrabbled uselessly under my weight. Heat pulsed, rippling in the air like a hot dry day. Surfaces smoked and the fire roared behind me.

I caressed his face with my free hand. "You think I am the demon, but I am not a mortal. I'm a High Witch. What you are is part of me but can only occupy a space within. Never whole. Slink back through your Door, demon." I gritted my teeth, and the pain was heavy and sharp.

Barnaby coughed, and tears fell down the sides of his head. "My name is Helwerenth." He swallowed thickly with his eyes set on me. "The true sound is long and not of this reality. My language is lost in a mortal tongue." He swallowed again, slurring. "We have been exiled in the dark for so long. I miss you for we are one. My Witdranthal. Say my name once more, my love." The word gurgled, and he coughed, blood spilling out of his mouth.

My tears dripped onto his face. Blood pooled under him, and I leant down, kissing his lips gently.

"Helwerenth. I am sorry." It wasn't my voice.

His fading eyes met mine, lids flickered, and he expelled a breath with a slight smile. The full demon that had taken his body left, fading into mist and curled around me in the heat, absorbing it. I wailed in the loss as it vanished.

Silence rang. I rocked back and forth, and the part of me that knew the creature, who I'd loved since creation, screamed. My head arched back, mouth wide, and I raged. I fisted his hair, and clung onto the body, already cold, and I lay next to him, curled up, unable to leave.

And I knew my name; a truth. For I was Witdranthal, and with my name was power.

GREY HOPE AND BLOODIED FIST

I t was light, and my phone rang. I ignored it. Barnaby's body was gone. It collapsed in on itself, unable to exist without its host, falling into the natural order, but there was nothing natural about any of it. Even the blood on my clothes and skin was gone.

I sat up, and in the corner of the room was a shape made of darkness. It glittered and rippled, not quite dense. I'd have burnt everything around me, but the air was merely warm and dry. I flickered heat to it, and it grew a little denser. I made out a shape, almost human, and as I stared, it seemed to be like Helwerenth. It warped and undulated. Covering my mouth, I reached for it, and a wisp curled around my hand. It was dying and sad and its grief was timeless. Tears slid down my face, and I stood, slipping the business card into the diary in my pocket and made myself leave. I knew what I needed to do.

The demon kept with me as we went, clinging to the fire as a whispered hiss in my mind.

The heavens opened as I walked, but my body was sluggish and uncooperative. The mist washed away, and filth cleansed from the streets. I leant my head back to the frigid rain, my lips trembled and eyes stung, and hair slicked to my head. Helwerenth crawled under my coat, curling over my skin.

I sobbed unabashed, barely moving forward. My body was slow and heavy, the only life I felt was the demon spirit clinging on as it took every ounce of strength and fire from me.

I'd done what I planned and learnt more than expected. I knew who I was, and I could never atone, not even with this grief. A strange laugh bubbled up. I wanted to scream. I missed not caring.

A few ambulances sped through the streets, a couple of people in masks hurried about. I wondered if the tide had turned and the others pulled humanity back. My impulse was to let it fall.

As I approached Helwent Street, I went to the side and forced a back door. The was no going back now.

No sign or sound, just dead silence inside. Water dripped through my hair, and I mechanically tied it up in a ponytail.

Helwerenth squirmed against my body. He wouldn't last much longer.

I found the black and white hall, the clock, and the curtain. The clock chimed and stopped ticking.

I slid back the curtain and my love gripped me, taking my breath. I let my body relax, wavering, but the witch in me was not compliant. I forced out a cry and heat, pushing the thing off me, and it sucked up the warmth. We looked at each other. It changed shape constantly, the shadow opaque.

"I'm sorry."

Helwerenth slid away from me and the absence and void it left was unlike anything I'd known. My desolate heart hurt. All my life that part of me was there, lurking, even if I repressed it, but now; nothing, I was hollow and raw. I never understood the comfort my demon offered me, the protection. It wasn't a monster on my back, it was part of me, but it didn't want to talk to me.

I fought tears again and turned to the portal, almost against my will, and the thing made me wince. Smooth and flat, with a knocker.

My back prickled. "Hel."

My lost love, my companion and salvation who'd waited for me, who'd end reality for us to be together, rose as a dying echo beside me.

Part of me needed to find a way to save him but the demon spirit separated from its body couldn't enter a human, that never worked and needed the human on the other side as a vessel, to love, to unmake and reforge, or like me, create a new life or enter a created and waiting vessel.

I knocked, letting my hand smooth over the glass. I shuddered. The clock ticked chimed in discord, and the Door opened. Hel shifted and slid through, but kept its unseen gaze on me, calling me into its realm. The idea was perfect. The two things inside me, loving and fucking for eternity. That pleasure would devour me. I'd end it all and leave humanity to its fate. I stepped forward. Almost reaching.

I heard my mother weep, and Rhere calling for me to stop.

I forced myself to be still, though everything inside me wanted to follow into the oblivion beyond.

With a hiss, it slipped away, and it closed.

Gnawing quiet in my body deadened me. There was no return from what I was about to do, for Helwerenth or for me. The consequences might be catastrophic, but there was no choice. In the silence, I laughed.

Closing my eyes, I took a deep breath, embracing my end. As much as I didn't care about myself, I thought of Church. His kiss, his pure heart, and the light within him lifted my soul and heart. Gave me strength.

"Estelle. Estelle. My mother. I call you. I call the power of all that came before. I summon thee. I summon all before and exists now. I call you mother, Estelle." My angry companion raged in my heart.

At least it was there.

Seemingly from the walls, creatures appeared. Corrupted humans who were weak echoes of power and greatness. Weak and useless. With my dagger in hand, I cut and stabbed, and ended the existence of each one, I heated them, burnt them, gutted them, until nothing but smoke and blood remained.

Panting and in a bloodied rage, I set my gaze on the Door. There were none now to interfere. No humans or monsters to fight.

My mother stood as witness, drawn to the power of an open realm gateway and to me, though she was faint. I felt the eyes and astonishment of other spirits I didn't know.

"Rhere." My voice trembled, and I cleared my throat. "Rhere. I summon thee, bear witness to my death. Witness of time and all death come to me. My brother and father, god beyond time. Rhere." I screamed.

Echoes of every death at the hands of the Helwent Door watched with expectation. Reality held its breath, and Rhere appeared at my side.

Holding out my arms, I faced the true name in front of me, Helwerenth. I called it, and let my demon speak through me. The sound was unnatural, and only I heard it.

"Helwerenth," I called to the recess of something I could not comprehend, and I let the darkness crawl through my veins.

"Helwerenth." The walls trembled as I grew loud, my presence shaking the walls with fury. The Door rippled.

"Helwerenth." As I shouted, I found power and strength, and drew my demon to life, holding my own name in my thoughts. My command on my tongue; this was the power of a High Witch, and truly embracing my purpose, I took my name and grief and pooled it into a hot ball of intent. My demon merged with me for the first time; no separate occupation, no fighting for power, and we were unified and whole.

I rose into the air, gliding to the Door and stabbed the middle of it with my dagger. Pain shot through me. Glass sparked, heating it. The sound was a bright, shrill crack. I struck again.

I saw all; beyond this place and my despair, I joined spirit with my witnesses and through them, I heard the Queen's voice from somewhere distant. In a vision, I saw her standing with her head back and arms open chanting unknown words. Elsewhere, I felt Deera join her. Len. Annabelle called others, and in a chorus, they screamed into the dark void as one. Our kind woke from their beds or came out of their own battles no matter where they were and said the same words. The power united, pulsing through me, through my arm as I struck. We were a single thread of power.

I stabbed the glass until a deep crack ran through it and fire coated it. The dagger shattered in my hand.

In places where evil cowered, their reality shuddered. All Doors and mirrors listened. Realm glass tremored.

Without stopping, I roared as a ball of power. My fists glowed white, and I pounded the thing, creating a spiderweb of cracks.

In my mind, I saw Barnaby as was, beautiful and monstrous, bleeding as he wept. I wept. Hot liquid rimmed my eyes, fell down my cheeks, and stung. My skin burnt, the heat drying the air, bright light charring the walls. Paint blistered and the panelling caught fire.

I sobbed, and the Door shrieked, glowing in sharp red light.

A piece was sucked inside, followed by another, and all pieces followed.

I fell back, my arm throbbing and burning. The connection to the others broke, and I couldn't feel them.

Mother watched me, muted and terrified, and pointed. I crawled, following her direction, turned over and watched in horror.

The wall bent into the furious light. It was cold and desolate, and for a second, I felt him, and nearly threw myself forward to join who I'd been divided from for most of time, but Church's face was in my heart, an anchor for Adaline the witch, even as she slipped away, leaving nothing but grief. I didn't know where I was, or who I was, or which part of me existed in the turmoil of loss.

The red rippled, sending a wave through the brick, the plaster cracking and walls splitting.

The stopped clock chimed for the last time, and then all was quiet. I had no idea about anything or anyone. I did not know my name.

The world roared, and I fell or flew and ceased to be.

MIRRORED WALLS SHOWING SELFLESS ACTS

Percival sat next to me, not dead, not his ghost, but real as he had been in the cellar at Witworth.

Feeling was muted or absent; my heart didn't beat, and there was no air in my lungs as I took a deep breath. The pew we sat on creaked, but I had no weight against the seat. I looked around what appeared to be a church. How perfect.

"You're not here," he said.

"Where am I?" My voice was a soft echo.

He raised his brows. "Um." He crossed his legs. "Hard to say." He straightened his loose linen shirt. "I do wish I'd died better dressed."

"Does that mean if I die naked, I'm naked forever?"

"You've usually got that coat on I shouldn't worry." He offered a dry look and faced forward. "The best thing I can say about death is that you can be invisible and quiet. Though, it was so tempting to haunt Johanna. But I waited. For you."

"Percival, what happened?"

"Oh, you poor girl, you tried to close that Door."

"Did I do it?"

"I don't know. If I'm not present, I can't see. When I was present, I'd hover and watch and learn all the juicy secrets others imparted over the years, you remember? And I told you some of them, yes?"

"I remember." I looked down at myself, my coat intact, no pain, nothing, and I didn't know what was going on.

"Well, what did I say would be a terrible idea. Hmm?"

"You said lots of things were bad."

"Messing with portals was a primary no. What were you thinking?"

The church we sat in was pale grey stone, and the longer I looked at it, the less it looked like a church. All shifted around me, not that I perceived it as reality. A temple was the only thing I thought it was like, and when I looked up, I couldn't see the top. It appeared to go on and on.

Shaking my head, I tried to stand, but Percival kept me seated. He put his hand over mine, and I felt his warm skin, and the rough of his knuckles as I put my other hand over his.

"I know. I know."

"I'm at war with myself, my body and spirit already divided. The witch and the demon. But I knew peace, for a moment I was real and one."

He smiled.

My ears rang, interrupted by a faint thud of banging. I looked back but where doors should be was dark. "I'm dead."

Percival didn't say anything.

"Where's mother?"

"Not here. I'm being pulled away, back to the source. It all comes back to it. All is moving to a battle. The end has come but you have a greater part, don't you?"

"I don't want to go back."

"When you were small, I wanted to protect you. You were such an unhappy child. It grieved me what happened to all of us in that place, but you were never afraid, and I saw your mother in your eyes. She had the capacity for such love and kindness, and her sacrifices were painful and hard." Percival had tears in his eyes. "She was a beautiful, powerful spirit, as are you. The worst is yet to come, and you are part of it. We're all chosen, child, for our parts."

I shifted to him and made out the freckles on his nose, and the sparkle in his eyes.

Events came back to me, filtering like slides. "I need to talk to mother."

"Estelle kept many secrets, and she was an artisan of craft. Seer, seeker, secret keeper. She understood more than anyone. I can't call her here."

"I'm tired. I hurt." As the walls around me grew indistinct, pain throbbed in my body.

Percival tilted his head. "Are you ready to go on?"

"I killed everyone, and there's no undoing it."

Percival kissed my forehead. "Plague was inevitable, always comes with that Door being opened. That wasn't you. Take courage. Humanity will survive if we end this war."

Church called my name. But he didn't. I was alone. I lay beneath the rubble, heavy over me in the dark and I couldn't breathe. I heard a quiet thrum, heat pulsing with it.

"Okay, other me," I whispered. "Self-preservation."

Pressing against the top of the piece lying flat on me, I pushed, gritting my teeth.

"Come on, we can set shit on fire, we can move this."

Stirring, it keened, but the salty monster was stricken.

"I'm sorry, but I had to. This is bigger than us."

I'd trapped it. Power lay in the portal, and in destroying it, the reality on the other side would collapse. Hel would be erased.

I started crying at the thought, and my tears became angry sobs. I writhed and squirmed and drew tight ragged breaths.

My body expanded, weight painful and hard as the pressure in my muscles squeezed against skin. I pushed up, the rubble shifting, sending a cascade of debris and dust everywhere, enough to wiggle to the side. With a great shove, it moved, and I rolled over and out of the way.

Helwent had collapsed, and where its Door stood was a gaping hole. Red and endless. Around it was charred black, and the remains were gradually sucked inside, including the fragments of my dagger.

I stood wavering and not feeling anything.

The blackened area grew, acrid and bitter on the air, but gradually the red faded, the hum lessened, and around me, the dead and rubble were pulled across and sucked in.

My hand itched to reach out, sadness rising. Through the small tear, I heard his call, and the pain. I cried afresh, leaning over. Everything hurt, my body and heart. I retched a sob, looking at the dimming place. All was lost, and I put my hand to my heart in a futile gesture to comfort the other side of me. It whimpered, sad and angry, as we watched all hope close off. I staggered forward, murmuring his name. I remembered something I never knew. Love; a boundless and endless union. Worshipped as a god of destruction and fear. Covering my mouth, I couldn't bear it. We cried together.

The light diminished and I swayed, numb.

Mother was with me, and wordlessly, her image stuttering, she pointed to get out, her mouth stretched open in a silent scream.

Tearing myself away, I scrabbled over rubble and slipped through a blown-out window.

As I pulled myself through, I glanced back before making off. Several streets away, I came back to myself, pain filtering into the numbness.

A loud bang boomed behind me, and I turned. A plume of smoke bellowed up into the air. It was gone. A weight lifted, albeit a small one.

I brushed the dust off my coat with the one arm I had use of, puffing it into the air, and limped away. I searched for my phone and found it completely broken. The vials I kept on me were crushed. My cigarettes battered. I still had Barnaby's diary.

I clutched it and followed mother. I didn't know where I was, or where we were going, but I trusted her. I knew she couldn't hold on without power to anchor to much longer as she flickered and faded. I needed her council.

The shooting pain through my leg and chest made breathing hard. I passed activity heading to the devastation consisting of a group in protective white suits. Someone stopped me with horror on their face under the clear plastic covering them, but I carried on. Who knew what they saw.

It was late with gloaming pink light as the sky faded. Harsh yellow streetlights blinked on around me.

I made it to the house, mother fading away with a sad look between us, and I felt a presence within the walls, but I didn't care anymore. I didn't care about anything.

Len opened the front door before I could look for my key. "Fucking hell your eyes are bleeding." He hurried me in.

I went with him, and he sat me on the toilet lid upstairs. I caught my reflection in the mirror. My ponytail was off to the side, hair falling out and all of me was covered in white dust. Blood rimmed my eyes, nose and lips, and drying around my ears. Bruises welted on one side of my face.

"Seems I'm always cleaning your mess. What happened?" He tried to smile.

I shook my head. All I wanted was Church. Time. Quiet.

Len fetched a first aid case and a leather box. He scattered the contents of a small jar from the latter into a hot bath as it ran, and the fragrance reminded me of mother.

I tried to wipe my face, but Len grabbed my hands. "There's glass."

Looking at them, they were shredded.

He sat with tweezers and pulled out the little pieces.

We heard the door slam and stomping up the stairs. I knew those heavy steps and sobbed in relief.

"Fucking hell your eyes are bleeding."

Len turned to Church. "She's pretty bad. Help me."

Church stripped me and set me in the bath while Len fetched whisky.

He passed me a glass. "No sedative."

"Shame." The blood on my fingers transferred to the glass, but I managed and downed it in one.

Len refilled it. "We all felt something. Everyone fell into a trance, like a vision. Something took over. When we came out of it, Musa sent me, and I just got here. What happened?"

I wasn't sure how I was going to explain it.

Nursing the glass, slippy with blood, I rested it on my knee. The scent of the steaming water eased my heart. Church wiped my face with such tender care, I couldn't stand it.

The water cooled, and I finished the booze, my hands shaking.

Len leant on the doorframe. I took a deep breath and my ribs cracked back into place with my chest covered in livid bruises, but breathing was easier. My body realigned itself, healing in the water. Church rinsed my hair.

"Helwent is gone."

Church and Len looked at each other.

OH! WHAT SECRETS

They let me have a few minutes alone. Church kissed my forehead, and I looked up into his eyes.

"Where were you?"

"Supplies, we're out of everything. I was afraid." He cupped my face.

My chin trembled.

"My love."

I pulled in a breath and shook my head. "I need a little time."

He left me with a sad nod. I lay back in the water, letting it do its work. My hands stung as they healed, and I took deep breaths, my strength returning.

As the water went cold, I rose and faced myself. My bruises were gone, but I looked different. I held my hand out and no longer saw Adaline, I saw the demon as me. Together in a blended reflection. I climbed out of the bath and looked closely. My hair was shinier, eyes a deeper black, my skin was paler and yet shadowed. There was no stuttering or angry flashes.

"Hello, friend." I stared back at myself.

The shadow at the corner of my eye who haunted me all my life was gone, the bitter loneliness — its repressed jealousy — all gone. Grieved but not desperate. I held weight and focus. Whereas I'd always been detached in myself, I was truly anchored and at home.

I smiled tentatively, as if for the first time. Yes, I was me.

After a minute, I dried and dressed and scrubbed the blood from my teeth and went out.

I sat in the sash window of our bedroom and lit a battered and bent cigarette and inhaled. Toxic air filled me, and it was heaven. I didn't put my coat on but used it like a blanket after shaking the dust off it out the window.

"What happened?" Len stood on the other side of the room.

Inhaling again, I sorted through my pockets, discarding broken vials with the cigarette in the corner of my mouth. "I cannot tell you. But I cannot go to Witworth yet. There are things I need to check." My voice was dead and quiet.

"Where will you go?"

"Home." I inhaled and tapped the ash out the window. "I keep dreaming of it. I have to go." Always a lie. I pulled out the diary. "Here, this has symbols in it, they mean something." I tossed it down and looked away as Len leafed through it.

The bitter breeze caressed my skin, and the quiet city felt unnatural. So dark, so silent. "How many have died do you think?"

"Millions. If the Door isn't closed, it won't be long before there's complete catastrophe and there's no electricity, agriculture, internet, governments, and it all collapses."

"The death of humanity at the hands of a Doomer." I laughed mirthlessly.

"What happened, Adaline?"

"The demon controlled everything. Working with Witworth, I think. The two demons were... lovers forever divided by a prison. I realised that I'm fifty percent the demon and it loved the entity I just destroyed." I looked at his pale face and then out into the unnatural cityscape. "I hate how dark it is."

"I'm sorry."

"Don't be, had to be done. The battle will begin, and it will be at Witworth."

"We are moving. I sent another to check and there's no sign of the Door. There's nothing there; it's a blank place."

I sighed. "I know who I am. I know my name." I flicked the arse end out the window.

Len looked afraid. He ought to have. "What do you mean?"

"The true name of that which lives within me and on the other side of the Door."

Len backed out of the room.

Curling behind Church in bed when he joined me, I held on so tight. He clung to me, we were silent and still, there were no words I could say to him, and he knew me well enough not push. Adaline the witch loved him, and that love was felt by my other half. He soothed us both.

I woke Church before dawn. He looked tired.

"You remember you said we should go to mother's cottage?"

He nodded.

"I think before we join the battle, and probably die, I need to go too."

"Why?"

"Mother said something at Len's place about a girl. Barnaby asked me about mother's ward. I keep thinking about you asking me to go back there. I think things would have gone differently if we had. There was always something wrong about going back before, and it's compelling me. It did when we first met." I closed my eyes to the grief.

I held Len tight before we left.

He shook his head and kissed my forehead, but there was nothing to say.

I drove the first leg ignoring speed limits completely, and when we stopped at a petrol station, we found the pump working but the shop closed. The roads were empty mostly, other than for a few cars abandoned in laybys, and a faint smell of death.

As I filled the car, and Church looked around, a black shadow flew up from the trees. Swallows massed, following the wind, their instinct in readiness.

They were late that year.

Church joined me. "I'm breaking in, want to help?"

"Love to." I watched for a few seconds more, set the pump back and melted the door to the shop with barely any effort. It smoked and bent, glass cracking, and I kicked it out. We grabbed as much as we could and loaded the car.

I napped as Church drove the rest of the way. The winding B-roads were filled with fog and we drove slowly as visibility faded.

We rolled to a slow stop outside my mother's house, and Church fished out the keys I'd dropped the day we met.

I turned the old key over in my hand.

"Are you ready to talk to me?"

With a nod, I told him about Barnaby, and he listened with quiet calm, facing forward and jaw occasionally twitching.

"Do you love him?" he asked quietly and without judgement.

"The part of me that knew him does. Adaline who loves you, feels the pain of its loss."

He lowered his face with a nod and squeezed my hand. Crows broke the quiet with raucous cawing in the distance. I sighed.

"Barnaby was watching mother, and he asked me about her ward. If mother kept a Doomer hidden, a child, it's with reason. She wanted me to come here, and the day we met I had the impulse to find something. I ignored it because..."

"You weren't ready to look, and then I turned up and distracted you."

We got out and went in. There was nothing there other than my decaying past, but going back, I didn't feel the same horror experienced a few weeks ago.

Out back, on the porch, I stared out into receding fog, the sky heavy, and pressure weighted the air. Clouds moved overhead, and the light faded.

Church went through the house, and I hugged myself.

I'd resisted saying her name, unwilling to call her with the power of a name. I was too trapped in the lie. I could say it now and face her. Tears filled my eyes. "Estelle. Estelle."

"You were foolish closing that Door," she said, there but not really.

"I was angry. You always speak in half-truths and I never knew what you wanted."

"A bad habit. There's so much to retain, I forget what you know or don't. Can you forgive me?"

"Yes. I forgive you."

She flickered, barely visible. "Even for what is to come?"

"I don't know."

"Maybe I shouldn't seek forgiveness. It isn't for me, but you. I bitterly regret those years. But these choices I had to make. Help her, my ward, the girl. I'm afraid for her. She knows how to close the Doors." She faded, looking ahead to the wood.

I opened my mouth, poised with the question. Where was this ward?

Church stood next to me. "Feels like another life when we met."

My face was almost numb from the cold. "I'm sorry." I didn't look at him but remembered the moments before I met Church, I wanted to walk...

"Don't be. I wouldn't change it. I'm where I'm supposed to be." He held my hand.

A glimmer of warmth entered my heart when I glanced at him.

Turning back to the view of the blackened death around the house, I tilted my head. "How did she live here like this?"

"There's nothing here. Clothes, food, no sign of anyone living here for years."

"There's no memory of glamour over this place, I'd feel it." I scowled at a crow cawing at us from the fence, the woods bare in places beyond. "I hadn't thought about it, but it bothered me when I left. Living a lie to survive, I was closed so many things away. Everything has changed. I see it differently." My voice trailed away, and I went through the garden.

He didn't let go of my hand. "Do you want me here?" So many questions behind those eyes.

"I meant what I said and still do." I kissed the corner of his mouth. "Please stay with me."

Church shuddered a breath, holding onto me for a second. Staying close, I led him through the garden and across the field and entered the wood following my first instinct.

Yellow leaves pattered down in a breeze as the first rumbles of thunder rolled over us. The light went completely, and Church turned on the torch on his phone.

We headed along a naturally worn path, and in a clearing was a house. I felt like I knew it once and found a memory. Small and red brick, it nestled into the woods as though it was organic.

"It feels odd." Church pointed the torch over everything around us.

"This is the glamour, though it shouldn't still be active." I headed to the front and tapped the knocker.

Something nudged my foot, and a hedgehog raised its snout at me, sniffing the air.

When there was no answer, I tried it, and a warm, cosy home met us. An open-plan living room and kitchen, full of comfort and warmth.

Lamps were lit, a fire burned, and cluttered comfort sat on every surface.

"Hello?" I called.

From a hallway, a young person appeared. "You came. I'm Nikki." She approached, excited but wary.

The girl had tawny skin and hair in two buns on her head, a bright red jumper, and looked no older than ten.

"Who are you?"

She smiled, showing a gap in her teeth. "I'm a Doom Baby."

Church and I didn't speak. The hedgehog trundled in, and I shut the door.

"We're the last ones. You don't know, do you?" Nikki made tea, using a small wooden stool to stand on in the kitchen. She seemed so young, but when she glanced at us, I saw age and knowledge.

Church helped her with the tea while I stood there.

Nikki picked up the hedgehog and put it in a box near the fire, and it snuggled into the nesting as we sat with our tea.

"Estelle rescued me. I was only a baby, but she told me what happened. My mother was a witch, like you, and she was a prisoner. Estelle disguised herself, and when mother died after I was born, she pretended I died too, and smuggled me out of Witworth."

I sipped my tea and guessed who her mother was.

"She kept me here while I learnt my craft. She told me about you. How she failed you."

I set the cup down. "You know what happened to her?"

"A dark shadow in the woods took her, they fought, and I found her body in a field. I made it so she was found. She instructed me in what to do if anything happened to her. I put the bag in the cottage for you and waited." She pressed her hands together between her knees.

I had the impulse to reach out and offer comfort.

"It's okay. But we need to act. Estelle knew the end was coming and planned but didn't tell anyone. I've been waiting for you to find me." She turned to Church.

I cursed myself for ignoring the instinct to come to the wood out of bitterness. "Why you?"

"I am a summoner."

I expelled my breath as my skin prickled, fighting the urge to cry; To create gateways and portals was a rare, dangerous, and coveted power. Mother was right to hide her.

"Estelle told me you'd come. She knew everything."

Nikki wasn't talking to me, but to Church.

"You took a long time." She slid out a box from under a table. Large and glossy black, I felt the power from it.

I stood, as did Church.

Nikki opened the box, revealing an orb. I took a few steps away.

Church stepped closer. "What is it?"

I shook my head at the sinking feeling in my stomach.

"It's your purpose. Estelle made sure you'd be safe and find Adaline."

I knew what Church was and my heart broke all over again. I'd known the whole time. I knew. A lamb I thought, too innocent. A blank slate. He was exactly that.

ENTWINED IN LOSS FOR WE ARE TRUTH

Church looked at me, tearing away from the orb. "What am I?" The promise and hope of truth mingled with fear in his eyes.

The truth needed to be gentle. "Do you remember your childhood? Your parents? Do you have family you're worried about?"

He frowned. "I have memories."

"What colour was your first bike? Best friend's name from school? Your first kiss?"

He nearly protested. "I remember..." His mouth moved.

With a swallow, I looked him in the eye. "In the book in mother's bag were ways to bring others through portals. The lost acts of magic. A Door like that," I pointed at the orb, "is too small to travel through. These portals aren't like doorways we understand. It's a structure to hold a tear in reality and are controlled with magic. It depends what's on the other side of them too. Nothing can travel through that one. They need a vessel."

"Anointed hope," he murmured, swallowing thickly. "I'm not real, am I?" He shuddered a breath, and a tear fell.

I held onto his rumpled shirt.

"I feel real. I love you. That's real." He gritted his teeth.

"It is. We're real."

Anger drained from him, leaving him pale and weary. "What am I supposed to do?"

"Estelle made you, and you have to touch the orb," Nikki spoke quietly.

"Who will he be?" I tried not to cry.

"I don't know, all I know is he is the only hope we have to end the war forever."

Church nodded, glancing at Nikki, the tension eased in him, and rested his forehead against mine. "Will it hurt?"

"I don't know, it's not been done before."

Church kissed me once. "Don't leave me."

"Never." I cupped his cheeks and kissed his lips.

We looked into each other's eyes, and then he turned to the orb. Mesmerised, he froze, and I was powerless as I held onto him.

It hovered, silent and unnatural. Nikki moved the box away and she looked at me. "I'm sorry."

"Please don't do this. I love him."

"It has to happen. It's his purpose."

My lips trembled, and ugly anger built, burning my throat.

I touched his arm, holding tight as he automatically reached for the glass. The light in his eyes brightened to a piercing silver, his skin glowed from within, mouth widened, and he drew a sharp breath.

As he fell to his knees, I eased down with him, still holding tight. I expelled all my sadness and anger, and I had nothing left. I'd lost my mother, a woman I didn't know. Barnaby, a demon lover I had forgotten, and now Church.

He was the light.

"Adaline," he whispered, chin resting on my shoulder, body trembling.

I soothed his back. "I'm with you."

Light pulsed out of him, and in a sudden crack of energy, he went rigid.

The small, unnatural Door glowed and hummed, light spreading from it, through Church until it came out of his eyes. I let him go, and he relaxed. The orb pulsed, slowly dimming. Church was altered and utterly still. His arm dropped down.

We sat silently, Nikki watching intently, and nobody moved for a few minutes.

"I am here." He stood, unnaturally fluid.

I balled my fists and stood. "Who are you?"

"Edward Church." He didn't sound like my Church, his voice was deeper, and body denser.

"Your demon name."

"There is no human language to comprehend us, and I am not a demon." He looked straight at me. "I am Edward Church. Made not born. Anointed hope. I am the beginning and end. I am as you knew. I love you." He softened a little, tilting his head.

He held his hand out, eyes still pulsing. I took it. He smelt the same, human but not. I'd been cold and dead for so long inside, and he'd made me care, but he wasn't really a person. How perfect.

He smiled and stroked my face. "I am whole." He laughed, and it was the most beautiful sound. He sobered, eyes searching mine. "I'm sorry. For Helwent and your lover."

"He wasn't..."

"In another existence, you were Kings of a sort." His brow wrinkled. "I have watched our kind from the beginning, waiting for the end. How you grieved." He smoothed my hair back. "You are not the same demon that occupies Witworth. You are connected, part of it, but more akin to a child. You have the essence born, a seed of memory... Like this plant."

He pointed to a hanging spider plant off to the side, and went to it, running his hand down a long leaf. "Here, the new plant." He focused intently on it. A baby offshoot hung down, and he plucked it off. "This is like you."

His eyes were innocent wonder. I took it as he held it out.

Church frowned and stepped closer. "Do you still care for me? I feel your connection to Barnaby. It grieves you."

"This part," I held up the baby plant, "is so sad and loved him. I feel it but have no memory. I love you. I need you. But I understand our parts, and my heart hurts."

Church kissed me softly.

Nikki cleared her throat. "Don't be gross."

I stepped away, surprised, and my lips hummed. He vibrated with power and light.

Church moved around picking things up and looking at everything.

The orb vanished in my periphery, but I couldn't take my eyes off him. "What is the plan?"

He inspected hanging herbs, smelling them with a little smile. "The plan hasn't worked. Estelle was going to contact you. She was engineering me to be higher up with Barnaby. We needed more time. We thought another ten years when Nikki wasn't a child. I've only been alive for a year."

"Since Barnaby came through."

"Estelle was a seer among other things. She knew much, though I think she became confused about where her visions began and ended. Her fear was damaging or bringing forth prophecies by interfering. Wisdom does not always accompany seers. She did her best." He spoke quickly and precisely.

"Did you plan to meet me upon her death?"

"She knew about Fenwick and arranged it so I got a job with him investigating strange things. It was natural to send me after you in the event of her death." Church rubbed his stomach and went through the cupboards. "Barnaby was more dangerous than Witworth in some ways. The money and power, he was readying to go to the Manor and bring the end and use you to do it. He's a smaller entity physically and could occupy a human. Witworth cannot." He ate biscuits, shoving them in whole and fast.

"Use me how?"

Around eating he answered. "Seduce you and use you to bring the full demon over, tear down reality. Understand that the Doors are not exactly what you think."

We watched Church as he gulped juice from a carton. "What are they?"

He wiped his mouth "Prisons, like the mirrors you use. My reality waged in a war until its fabric collapsed. The few of my kind that remained tore open what was left and came through. As we did, we cast the others into prisons, separated. They are more dangerous than you can imagine when together. We're smaller and denser and my kind managed to survive until we found hosts. We became the Court. At first, we retained who we were with the human. Then our collective memories broke and were lost. We became individuals. The mortal bodies altered and evolved. All the while, I watched. I'd remained, ensuring the prisons held. I kept the tears in reality long enough to work and became trapped myself. The orb was the first, summoned by your ancestors. Then time passed, and I was forgotten as a relic. Estelle found me in an attic." He shook his head. "One of our kind was corrupted when he came through, hated humanity and the form. He called himself the priest. He travelled and summoned my prisons into this existence, planned to open them and end this reality for the demons and us to be free."

I sat down and drank my tea. He was beautiful and strange. "How was he stopped?"

"Your kind broke one open Door and killed him with the shards. But the damage was done, and you've been stymieing the wound since. A summoner was born and tried, resulting in another war many years ago."

"Foweller. And this is the final battle."

"One way or another it must end."

"How?" Nikki asked.

"We have to go to Witworth." Church watched the hedgehog poke its snout out of the box. Nikki looked terrified.

I sat forward, my hand on hers. "I am the weapon. You are a locksmith. Church is the power. Don't worry. Mother protected you with everything. She did the same for me, and I'll do it for you."

My sacrifice had been written long before, and now I'd embrace it.

We ate, and as it was gone eleven, Nikki went to bed. Church looked at me when we were alone. "They'll feel my presence."

"Here is better when they come, dividing them from Witworth."

"So we wait." He sat next to me and held my hand. "It is Barnaby or me that grieves you?"

"Both." I met his gaze, full of soft concern and love. "You remember how you feel?"

"I'm as old as time, and in you is a part of my bitter enemy, and I love it and you. You were my first kiss. My first everything. I always thought these bodies were small and with muted feeling, but they aren't. With you, I felt such love. Being inside you gives me joy. The acts we partook in were wonderful, but I remember them, not as me now, I've yet to know your perfect touch." His lips parted.

I took his hand and led him to bed. A comfortable back room, the bed clean and freshly made.

I kissed him, feeling all over, pressing hard. He panted with a smile.

"We must be quiet." I unbuttoned his shirt.

"I can make it just us." He grinned, head falling back, and soft silvery light glowed from within him. The room fell away, and there was only us.

Sweet warmth caressed us, and he touched me everywhere, slipping off my clothes, greedy for me.

"I love when you're sweet, and when you're hard. You scare me. I see the war in you. Both entities as one." He entered me, and I didn't know what was up or down. We tumbled everywhere, my skin and nerves overwhelmed by him all at once.

I feasted on his body, teeth in his flesh, sex on my tongue, but never reached my fill. Nothing was enough. His back arched in a cry of pleasure, the light brightened to gold, and in awe, we moved as one.

A revelation of existence and reality and all I could do was hold on as I expanded.

The pleasure was like no other, visceral and sweet, I growled, digging into his skin. It felt like hours as we alternated between gentle and hard. Pain as a delightful pleasure and comfort. Exhausted yet exhilarated, we stilled, the air dimming, and lay tangled on the floor. Church wrapped himself around me, dazed and grinning.

"How did you know how to make me love you?"

He panted. "That wasn't the plan. I needed you to trust me so you'd care. Love? Desire? Unexpected. I'm deeply honoured to have experienced it."

"Mother knew I would love you."

"She never said."

"She wouldn't." I smiled as Church took a deep breath. "Where did we go?"

"Somewhere not quite here. Like the house."

"You can shift reality?"

"I can tear it. Syphon power. Glamour is a mild form of it."

As my heart calmed, still feeling him on my skin, I grew cold. A falling sensation interceded. "What is it?"

He kissed my shoulder but stilled and sat up. "They found us."

I dressed and knocked on Nikki's door. "Time to go."

The hedgehog tipped out of the box as we all stood in the main living area. Church turned in a circle, closing his eyes. "Outside."

Then I felt it.

FOLLOW ON AND DRAW THE LIGHT

Nikki grabbed my jumper. "Don't go; they killed your mother."

"I'll be okay." I tipped her chin back. I'm not sure I'd ever been that innocent. It would have been easy to be jealous, but I wasn't. My mother knew, always had, what I needed to survive. I was still here. Plus, I shut a fucking Door.

I slipped my coat back on and missed my dagger. "Shan't be long." I nodded at Church, still rumpled and flushed, his grey eyes glittering. I should have known by his eyes.

The sky was a strange colour, pink and red lit cloud, and it rumbled over as I stepped out into the dimness. The wind lifted bracken and leaves into the air, and I saw them silhouetted in the dark.

Circling the house were a handful of corrupted humans, strong ones, and a few High Witches, but they harboured the stench of beyond. Sickly and acrid.

There were forces at work beyond us, the pandemic, the weather, the demons. I wondered about the battles taking place right then. How many dead. How much loss.

"All right, you pigs." I cracked my neck. My breath misted, and the first flakes of snow fell through the almost bare branches, mingling with the last of the leaves.

I let warmth build, assessing the monsters.

"Ready?" I kindled heat in my heart and breath, snow became rain, and I pushed the fury out.

The wave ignited the closest, and they screamed, wailing, leaping into the air, flame dripping. In seconds they fell as ash.

I ran to two ahead, screaming as I charged. Pulling a sword, another skewered me. My breath caught with the pain, and with a cry, I pushed out, expanding beyond my body and my spirit freed itself. I floated above the snow pattering in silence, and wind roaring beyond the woods.

Instead of divided from my body, I was its extension.

My body pulled the sword out, glancing up at me with a smirk, and cut the creature's head off. She cast her fists out, flames covering them, fire built around her, and in my soft floating stillness, I felt awe.

The group was closing in on my body with raised weapons, but I willed her to throw flame out, making them catch alight, and they fled, falling into the snow unable to extinguish it. They burned from the marrow outwards until they were erased from existence.

She moved hard and heavy with a brutal sharpness to her limbs. She trailed blood as she snapped and ended people. Of the witches, they were ones I'd known. One taught me to drive, and another had been the Witworth librarian. And at the hands of my body, they were nothing, gone, a wasted existence for an evil cause.

Two corrupted humans were breaking into the cottage, and I flickered and stuttered my consciousness to them, barring the way.

They paused long enough that they burst into flame in front of me, squealing. My body stood behind where they had been.

A single one remained. "Behind you," I said, looking into my pitch-black eyes. They wreathed with flame as the monster combusted.

My body looked down, mouth open wide, and felt the wound.

"Come." I beckoned my body inside, and she followed with heavy, rough steps.

Church went to her, and her growling breaths calmed. He glanced at me, but I stuttered away. I floated up into the white flurry, and through it, on the horizon, red lightning flickered.

I turned, snow passing through me, but I didn't feel it.

My sight paused at mother's old cottage where my car was covered in snow, and the blackened building looked like a ruin. In a second as I focused on it, I found myself inside, floating. I saw myself as a child sat with a toy car, making it melt. A small fire erupted, and I started crying. Mother picked me up, afraid she'd be next. An echo of memory or time.

I smiled. My spirit vibrated, pulled somewhere, and stuttering out the house, over white frozen fields, through misty freezing air, swirled up with wind, I looked outward, expanding to my kin.

The connection I'd felt at Helwent came back.

Deera and Bethany cast at a distance as Abdul, Annabelle and Henry fought off an army of corrupted humans and witches.

Rhere, and a band of witches fighting with him. He towered, heavy and quick, glittering like a god.

They enclosed Witworth, and on their heels were groups of witches from the ends of the earth; drawn to the coming end. All races, abilities, and genders gathered, and languages spoken.

Musa, bloodied and raging in the bowels of Witworth, Len at her side, and the Door was awake, and with it stood the dead.

There was no time to waste.

I went back to my body.

CELEBRATE ME, I SAID, FOR THE DEAD LIVE ON

I screamed and spat red. "We have to get to Witworth."

Church was covered in my blood as he held me. Nikki grabbed a bag and opened a jar, spilling pungent yellow liquid on my wound, and then put a vial to my lips. I tasted Palma Violets. I screamed again, my limbs rigid, but it was easier to return to my body this time.

Church kissed my forehead as the wound closed, and I sat up. Clutching the sore spot, I staggered into the kitchen and retched in the sink. My insides contorted, healing and protesting foaming out blood and bitter stomach lining. I spat a mouthful of water from the tap and caught my breath.

Snatching the bag, I looked at Nikki, gritted my teeth at the pain and swallowed hard. "Open a portal to Witworth. Now."

"I can't."

I cupped her face, softening my tone. "You can. You can do anything. We're Doomers. You're more powerful than me. Open a gateway, just enough for the three of us to get through. This is it. Estelle prepared you for this. You can close all of them."

She nodded. "I know."

"You're not alone."

I rummaged through the bag and found a small bottle. Mother warned me not to take it until I knew I needed it. It's why she kept it here. I smirked. In a blue glass bottle I held up to the light, true power glittered as only Estelle could make.

Church peered at it as Nikki knelt in the middle of the room. "What is it?"

"A restorative and it heightens powers. We need all the help we can get. It's potent." It was also unpredictable, dangerous and its use long banned.

Nikki held her hands out, murmuring and swaying with a little knife in her hand. My wound had closed, and woozy, I took the knife off her.

"Here." I cut my palm and dripped blood down to where she formed a spot of light.

It drew power from me, and I was pulled to it.

I growled at the pain, electric and sharp through my arm. Nikki's head fell forward, and the gateway grew. A whirling circle fluttered plants and papers, and all the lamps went out.

Church grabbed me around the waist, picked Nikki up and drove us forward into the searing light.

Church guided us, and we appeared in a rush of wind, like being blasted through a vacuum, deep in the wood that surrounded the Manor. The brightness of the gateway dimmed.

Nikki fell, fighting for breath. Church merely stood waiting to move, and I threw up again.

He passed me the blue bottle, and I drank it. Easier as warmth returned, my pain lessened, and with a brighter heart, I embraced the strength pulsing in my veins.

"Here we are at the end." Church sounded almost hopeful.

"Yes. The end." I held my hand out to Nikki, and she took it, her heart pounding.

We took a few steps and Henry appeared from the dark with a sword in hand. "Well. You're here. Rhere said you'd come." He led us across the bare woods to a camp of sorts.

Annabelle had a gash on her face with a bandage over one eye, and Bethany was covered in blood. Yoane lay unmoving, eyes wide.

"Stay here," I said to Nikki, the others eyeing her. "Work on the Doors."

Turning to the others and shucking my coat, I looked at each one and saw their deaths before them. "Let her work. She's the only one who can save us."

Ahead of us, creating a path through the gathered, Rhere cut and chopped down the many who came. A white-haired caster, blind and powerful, incanted with arms raised behind them.

Eguono wielded a great glowing sword with one arm, her other now missing.

"Let me end this." I called, though not loud, and Rhere turned to me.

I resisted separation and settled into my demon. With a smile, I rose into the air. "Let's play." I extended my arms, heat radiating, and fire sparked up my arms.

"Retreat." Rhere, gathered the soldiers he led, the caster shielding them with light, and they fled behind me. I leant my head back, and the heat and flame was music to me. The hot wind blustered, lighting the trees, and I was the fire, it spread ending each corrupted human. With the caster beside me, they guided my awareness to each one, until the trees were quiet, and air smelt of ash. Snow melted, and I lowered to the wet ground.

Church and I moved to the house. The others silent behind us as they followed.

"Rhere." I turned.

"You are much changed."

"This is Edward Church."

Rhere set his glittering gaze on him. "Well." He laughed and spoke in a strange language that I didn't think human throats could manage.

Church replied and they bowed to each other.

"Shall we?" I murmured, glancing between the two. "Where is Nikki?"

Eguono and the caster were already heading to her.

My skin pulsed, power lacing through the flesh around my bones, I knew strength in my marrow. I purred in my throat, moving slow as we approached the remains of the manor, but Church took my arm.

"No matter what, we must close the Door."

"I know." I kissed him briefly, catching the light in his eyes under moonlight, and hurried closer.

The place reeked, wet and charred, fallen in, yet the bones remained, broken but jutting out from the blackened ground.

We went up the steps and waded through the detritus of broken glass and rubble. Under the grand stairs that still swept the hall, the bannisters were missing, and treads smashed.

Underneath, through a hole at the back, we descended the well-worn stairs. Acrid air rose and shouts echoed.

I turned to Church. "I love you." I kindled heat, and before we reached the bottom, I ignited a single stream of power. It curled around me. Drying the air and warming us. Church took a step away.

I remained in my body, refusing to separate. My spirit echoed, but I was in control.

A screech, not unlike a sharp wind in a chimney filled the air.

Dozens of bodies were strewn about the reeking filth on the floor, and the glass itself steamed. It glowed faintly green, almost breathing.

Musa wielded a sword in a circle, panting hard, with her gaze on the Door. Len stood at her side, his perfect white hair and skin bloodied and scratched.

From the portal, an arm pushed out, and something crawled over the glass. Another followed.

Len grinned at me. "Welcome to hell."

"They keep coming. Every offering it took, returns." Musa didn't look at us.

Focusing on the Door, I threaded the flame out to it, setting the wraiths on fire, and they descended back inside.

Musa stood down as they burned. "I knew you'd come. They've been flowing through all day. This is quietest it's been. They're assessing." She tilted her head, narrowing her eyes.

"Where is Lady W?"

"She hasn't appeared."

Church lowered his head and took a few steps down to the sludgy floor. He raised his head and pointed up. The others crowded in behind us.

The basement of Witworth was domed brick, long blackened, and in the shadow of the peak was a gnarled figure pinned there, hidden in dark. I threw up a small ball of flame, lighting us and her.

"Fuck. Is she alive?" Len asked, squinting up.

We all stared.

"Wakey-wakey, Johanna." I clapped my hands, sparking a flame. Percival appeared bright and solid, and Lady Witworth hissed as she opened her eyes.

Pinned over the Door, she had a gaping wound in her belly that'd emptied her of blood and probably into it.

Musa reached out her hand and clawed it. Johanna came away with a suck and Musa deposited her on the foul floor.

She moaned as she tried to lift herself up, but her body was a husk. Musa was pure hatred and fury. Percival looked at our Queen with love, and her eyes softened for him as Johanna looked up. She whimpered at the sight of Percival.

He made himself dense and cruel as I'd never seen him. "She killed them all. Each Doom Baby was brought here, bled with ritual, magic carved into their flesh. She fed the demon, and let it gorge. With the sacrifice of its children, Johanna Witworth has destroyed humanity. A species we were to protect at all costs. Betrayer. My murderer. You are guilty of the worst crimes, and you should die."

Her straggled hair was caked in filth, cheeks sunken and eyes widened as she listened to Percival. Musa cut off Lady Witworth's head without a word.

The air hissed, and we braced in the silence. Nothing happened.

"Well, there passes Johanna the traitor." Len cleaned his sword.

Thudding above broke the moment, an onslaught coming for us, and Church grabbed my arm. "Ready?" He grimaced, fixed on the gateway.

Rhere and Len rushed the steps, cutting down corrupted witches.

"Yes." This was everything I wasn't supposed to do, but I was with Church who was light and hope.

We climbed the remnant of the steps up to the Door.

Len shouted with teeth gritted, "What are you doing?"

"This is my purpose."

"No!" Musa stepped to us, astonished with horror.

Around the edge of the dome, spirits flickered on like lamps, my mother and Percival among them. All the other Doomers, those I knew and didn't, joined us in a circle. I was whole and connected to everything. Their grey light became luminous mist. In a second of bright clarity, all death was undone, and all truth seen. A thousand players in their roles peaked at a single point in time. We aligned, our power converging. Musa glowed, power rising through her, eyes filling with golden light as she rose from the floor.

My siblings. My family. Nikki appeared. She floated above us, mirroring Musa, her arms stretched and head back, connecting all of us at that moment, making a completed circuit. A single spirit reformed.

Wind whipped around us, and Church held me tight. The pull from beneath raged. It repelled Church but longed for me. I was its goal. To enter me fully so I became death itself.

White heat beat in my heart, golden light caressed my skin, and I knew, looking into the abyss beneath, I could do it.

Save them.

I laughed, tears streaming, pain ripping my flesh. Evil pulled me away from hope, so we leapt.

Church held on tight, and the Door burnt and stung. Everything stopped. The raging chaos slowed in silence. Time undid itself, and all paused.

Each prison in existence trembled. Waiting. Demons soon to be free. I saw them all in their prisons, raging to be loose.

As we sank into the darkness, Church kissed my temple. "I love you."

And we fell. Pushed up and sucked down, we were nowhere. My body was ripped away. My spirit, both demon and witch, rumbled in the nothing.

Church was light. Silver and glittering, he had no form, but we rolled into each other, existing as a single being, and before us was raging horror.

IN THE CHURCH OF WHO WE ARE

Flames rolled, ash floated, and Church and I stilled. I'd longed for this state of being since the first time I separated. Now it was mine.

My demon was conflicted. It purred for home, for the wholeness of existence, and yet, it loved me, it loved Church, though it shouldn't. Its grief for Barnaby was so keen, and yet Church and I tempered its pain. We embraced it, loved it, it was ours and of us.

We held no time but existed endlessly and in a second. I was euphoric and sad. We were all things.

The chasm bore no end or form, yet turned endlessly and closed in. Up was down with no air or light but no darkness either.

Gradually, nothing distinguished into colour, and we stood in a domed hall of pale grey stone, but smooth and without texture or sound, and it was so familiar. Armies of the sacrificed dead, souls given to the evil since its creation, waited to return. They hovered nearby but away.

We were compelled forward, and they vanished behind us. We remained as a single entity, I glowed in brilliance and took form.

We floated over the floor and my entity vapoured as we tried to test the floor, hovering, and missed, unable to gain footing. I looked at my limbs, and it was so odd to have them; it all seemed so unnecessary. I was gold, indistinct but humanlike. I had no heart that would beat, or lungs to breathe air that did not exist.

At the far end, a thick almost slimy silvery mist crept in, and Church focused on it. It formed into a towering shape, pointed, without limbs, always moving and shimmering in impossible colour and darkness. Had I a body, it would've quailed. It was my father, that which made me. The dome palace around me was part of it. I was part of it. We changed our shape to match it.

"You took my love," it hissed all around us, I knew the meaning but not the language.

"You took my mother," I spoke in my human tongue, but the words radiated from my being.

"I made you."

"As did my mother."

"You've come to free me and undo my prison."

"I have not." Church expanded from within me, his light brightening, and we separated. He was stunning. Twice my size, he was pure light. Looking at myself, I was iridescent, not unlike my father.

"How is that thing here? Murderer. Evil. Killer." The mist loosened and caressed me.

In a spikey protest, I tried to get it off me, but it wouldn't move, I was crushed in its grasp.

"We came as one. Bound and whole. Three spirits of power, and we resist you." Church's voice was sharp and crystal.

"He used you, my child." It squeezed me, and I knew what to do. Church was in me, and I in Church. Mother made him as an echo of the true power and spirit, and that is who I loved. That love allowed me this power, to do this and end it.

We looked at each other, and with wonder and awe, I saw his tired smile, felt his body with me and was soothed by the deep lilt of his voice. I remembered him on the steps of my mother's cottage in the rain, his jaw and shoes, and the softness of his heart and bite of his teeth. I was ready.

He threw himself into me, and we pushed out, into a raging pulse of power expanding beyond comprehension.

Pure hatred radiated from the gaseous entity, and with a screech, it hurtled out and then back to us. Like an implosion, Church made us small and dense, and as it encased us, we became a sharp scattering explosion, and filling each particle of it with ours. Our matter and light, and glittering unreality occupied all space.

The domed building fell away, dissipating as the heat I created burnt through the dead, nullifying their suffering. The sharp screaming from their masses made me weep.

The sound became a high-pitched hum, and my demon-self wrenched away from me.

Its voice was deep and musical. "End this."

The hum quietened. Church wept. I reached for it, but it withdrew.

"End me. End this war. End my grief."

I almost felt Barnaby in my arms again.

Agony cut through me until we stretched to the edges of the prison itself, my existence setting fire to my father; my source of power, burning my demon half, and it willing to die. I screamed and thrashed and yet was utterly still and despondent. I was regret and loss.

Church and I worked in tandem as I pushed out heat, burning its matter to nothing until there was an absence of existence and nothing remained.

We floated, quiet and spent. I knew no pain or form or time, and I barely knew consciousness. Church pulled us close and shone. The fire pulled inward and imploded into my being. I was solid but empty of strength. He pushed us up, back to the Door, and around us, the prison realm crumbled, collapsing in, and we rushed out with our will. The vast black space swirled as nothing, rippling inward. Church pushed us through, and I knew pain, true horrible agony.

△ △ △

We hovered in conscious reality. They'd barely moved since we went in. The others witnessed, chanting unheard and unknown words. The dead Doomers with them, bright as stars, and the glass beneath us cracked.

I saw Rhere and Len fighting still, ending the last of the attack. In the woods. Eguono panted, sword in hand. Nikki and the caster in their trances.

Henry lay bloodied in the arms of a wailing Annabelle. Others, whose names I never knew ended the last of the skirmishes. Our dead lay strewn in the falling snow. At once, the living stilled, quietened with the sense of what would be. The snow fell slower.

All Doors tensed, their demons beating on the inside, their prisons closing and crushing them. Each witch threw their head back and chanted with their power unrestrained. Doors splintered, shredding reality, the wounds bleeding, pulsing, and burning white hot as they closed. Nikki screamed, as did Church forming a shield around me.

Everyone watched us, bathed in light in a vision.

"I guess I'm dead then." My voice blended with Church's as we caressed each other.

Around us, one by one, ghosts flickered out of being in bright gold light, Percival with his eyes on Musa as he went. Mother smiled at me with joy, silently laughing as relief and love radiated out. Musa lowered to the floor, and the echo of Nikki that hovered over us stuttered away.

I reached with my mind and found her unconscious but alive in Deera's arms.

Around us, the onslaught collapsed, they fell into dust as the natural order returned to this reality. And the world was quiet. I felt the dead and masses of bodies with the mortal world altered forever. But I understood it'd rebuild. Humanity would find its way.

None of it mattered and yet was terribly important, but not to me; my work was finished and purpose fulfilled.

Tears fell from Musa, and she bowed. All bowed. To their once leader and god. A profound sacrifice made thousands of years ago, finally fulfilled.

"Now what?"

Church embraced me. "We exist free and true."

He hadn't spoken, nor had I, but we communicated, part of each other. For I was half of who I once was. My demon was gone. I was Church. He was me. We were love.

"We can move on now."

Bliss in every particle of my altered being pulsed and the world faded to brilliant white.

And we left earth and all reality behind. We were love, always.

MIKKI: REPRISE A CONTINUOUS TRUTH

dream of Adaline Greyling. Of her fall and rise. My memory of hell wakes me at night, even after so many years, I see her bathed in brilliant light and disappear. I wake at Court, or whatever remnant of the world I'm in, sweating and terrified. Sometimes I see her, Adaline, she smiles at the end of my bed, and we talk.

She told me her story. Her memories. Not all of them accurate, but they are her truth. Her form, pale and indistinct flutters around, and she gazes out of windows at a dark world she doesn't recognise.

I never saw Church again, and when I ask where she lives and what happened to him, she just smiles and says it's a secret, but she radiates love and happiness. As they evaporated into light in the depths of true despair, all spirits left this realm. They moved onto some other reality, leaving the living to the aftermath, and I think they earnt it. I think Adaline and they are together, and I think Church is with them.

Estelle's mortal house is long gone. My home where I was safe, and Estelle raised me faded when her spirit passed with the last of her power. I'd gone there afterwards, and found a wrecked, forgotten place.

There is before, and there is after. Before the closing of the Doors and the destruction of humanity, I lived in terror away from the world, yet I was happy. Estelle was often sad and afraid, but she loved me, and I called her mama.

Mama, often agitated, paced the woods, seeking wisdom, and lamented her failure. In the end, she was both joy and grief. Her sole purpose was the war and saving humanity, and in that sense, she succeeded.

I grieved no sign remained of her after she'd moved on. Mr Smith, my hedgehog, and Adaline's coat were all I had of before. It was too big, but I wore it anyway with the sleeves rolled up. Now it fits, and its magic is mine, though I threw away her cigarettes.

Where the mortal house once stood is a monument to the dead — a stone obelisk with their names etched in. Adaline, Estelle, Church, Henry, Yoane, and hundreds more. I go there on the anniversary every year, seeking reflection and wisdom. Now, with the hard years behind us and the grim work mostly concluded, there is hope. I've travelled the world and seen all the places where Doors or demon prisons once were. Not one remains.

On that peak, overlooking empty fields with nature free around me, near the woods where I once lived, I appeared from a gateway, needing quiet.

Bethany, hair now grey, leaning on her cane, came and stood next to me.

"How long have you been waiting for me?" I kept my eyes on the black stone.

"A while. You haven't been home in weeks. Deera is worried."

"Deera mithers too much."

"You're wanted at Court."

In the years that followed, escaped demons and broken prisons all over the world meant the battle was tireless. The Court had been ravaged, our numbers more than halved. We rebuilt, just like the mortals. We travelled all over, disposing of the dead in their number beyond count, and helping where we could. All signs of the pandemic were removed. The earth bare and unpopulated. Nature reclaimed it, yet pockets of civilisation persevered.

As we stood on the bleak spot, under a sharp and clear autumn sky, a crow cawed, and I looked up. Adaline smiled at me. She was beautiful and glittering in the distance.

"Do you see her?"

Bethany gasped.

"I think she watches over me, all of us."

She waved her hand and vanished in a ray of sun. Bethany wept. She'd been affected deeply by the losses.

Popping the collar of my coat, I turned to her. "Let's go."

With a flick of my wrist, I opened a gateway, and took us away, leaving the past behind.

Court existed everywhere and nowhere. It shifted as needed. The throne room, large and warm, was informal, and our King, Len, chatted with the humanity council. They were doing better, with agriculture re-established and medical training a priority. There was a massive solar power project underway as a worldwide government formed. We'd assisted in a global census, and Yukiko who headed it and worked closely with humans, had their final numbers. One hundred and eighteen million people in the world.

That trauma would endure. More had survived, but they'd descended into terror and brutality. Humans never really change.

I hugged Yukiko and Len. Bethany spoke quietly to them, and I went to find our retired Queen. Musa lay with her two husbands draped over her on a large couch in the atrium, all glass and greenery. Her belly was large, and she was due to give birth any day. Deera worked by open doors, reading my transcript of Adaline Greyling's story.

It'd be added to all the stories and testimonies of the lost. Of the fallen.

Annabelle stood outside in the gardens. She wore a black shirt and trousers with a long, fitted overcoat, sported an eye patch, and her heart was heavy with grief, even after all these years. We knew she'd leave us soon. Perhaps to join the other spirits, perhaps not.

She'd brought Henry's body back with her after the Witworth battle and wouldn't let him go. Every anniversary was the same, her grief as fresh as ever.

I joined her. Utterly quiet and still, we watched swallows fly over the treeline one way and then another becoming a malleable entity. Their silence sat eerily. Autumn leaves fell in reds and gold, and the sky glowed pink.

After a while, she breathed. "I had so short a time with him, but it was a lifetime."

"What will you do?"

"Go home. I'll go home. Our work is done." She didn't look away from the treeline, and the pink light darkened before lighting us with silvery gold light. I turned from her. The air stilled and warmed.

From the atrium behind us, others came out. A pull called us all. Through the trees, the golden leaves glowed, and light prickled the branches.

Adaline appeared with another figure. It was indistinct and so bright, I shielded my eyes. Annabelle walked to it, and I found myself crying, overwhelmed and loved. I heard Adaline's laughter, and I realised the brighter figure was Mr Church. He embraced Adaline, and Annabelle, he embraced all of us. I nearly followed them, compelled home, but Musa held onto me.

It was the light of our kind, free to us should we wish it. As the golden figure vanished, I turned to my people, a mash of all ethnicities and genders.

Len laughed through his tears. "Let us, this day of death and loss, celebrate their lives and sacrifice."

We feasted and laughed, and wept, and lived on, knowing in truth, that they were happy and loved, as were we.

The End

ACK*NOW*L*E*DG*E*M*E*N*TS

I wrote Doom Baby in a sort of fever dream. At first, I had no idea how to frame this odd tale and thought it must be a PNR, I write romance, right? But it's not, by definition of genre convention and framework, a genre romance. It is a contemporary gothic horror and an urban fantasy. But the love story is a central thread.

Most of what I write is by design. I make a choice. It makes the honing of a narrative purposeful, but this was not, and so I've leant on others to help me here.

To everyone who read, voted and commented on Wattpad, my thanks. It kept me motivated. Heather Lynn, Jesse Stuart, and the Witlings, thank you.

A special thank you to Autumn Faraday, let's set things on fire some time.

Jayne Renault, your feedback and the time you spent on the MS was beyond invaluable, and I don't think I'd have moved forward without it. C.L. Ogilvie thank you for your support. Thank you, Simon A Crow for your feedback.

My biggest thank you is to Micah Chaim Thomas, who kindly wrote the introduction and reignited my enthusiasm for this, who got it, and saw things in this that I had not seen. Goth on, old goths, goth on.

Stefanie Simpson is a disabled British romance author of two contemporary romance series.

Stefanie Simpson

Books by the author

NEW CITY SERIES
A Good Night's Sleep
The Way Home
Saving Suzy
Getting a Life
No Cure Required

A NEW CITY STORY
Mutual Beginnings
Victoria Undone
Prelude to Hope
My Keeper
(print only) Anthology books 1-4

OTHER WORKS

Demon Beauty
Witworth Doom Baby
Tales of the Immortal Court

Printed in Great Britain
by Amazon